P.C.

X Nugget! ✓

The discovery of Colorado's largest ever gold nugget in Dirty Devil Creek precipitated a greedy confrontation that was to have far-reaching consequences. Journeying across the state to take possession of a family inheritance, Finn McCall, a dirt farmer from Kansas, finds himself languishing in jail framed for the murder of the old prospector who had found the nugget.

When Finn's younger brother learns that Finn is destined for the hangman's rope he knows it is up to him to rescue this innocent man.

But what chance does he have and can Finn's name ever be cleared? Will the nugget be returned to its rightful owner? These and many other questions must be resolved before justice can be done.

Nugget!

Dale Graham

A Black Horse Western

ROBERT HALE · LONDON

Typeset by
Derek Doyle & Associates, Liverpool.
Printed and bound in Great Britain by
Antony Rowe Limited, Wiltshire

ONE

DISCOVERY

Even with the temperature hovering at zero, sweat poured down the old prospector's grizzled visage. Wearily he heaved another load of gravel into the rocker cradle. A watery sun poked its golden orb above the surrounding peaks heralding the start of another day. It was hard work that only the toughest were able to stomach; an endless chore riffling for gold dust 'til the last vestiges of light disappeared over the scalloped horizon.

Yet already, Ezra Tindle had been at work on his claim for over two hours. He stretched his aching back, rubbing the soreness from muscles long accustomed to gruelling toil. Casting a jaundiced eye towards the canvas lean-to at the edge of the clearing, he snorted derisively.

Where in tarnation was that young pup? Sleeping off another drunken orgy, no doubt. The old guy had been fast asleep when Deakin had finally made it back to camp. The horse knew its way by now. Tindle was fast wishing he'd never taken him on as a partner. Curly Joe, as he liked to be called, had turned out to be a definite liability. Sure, you could sift through far more gravel when there was two of you. But that was only when that lazy turd made the effort to raise his goddamned ass.

This was the third time in as many weeks that the kid had made the half-day trip down to Telluride. Ostensibly to replenish their supplies. More than likely to toss what dust he'd found into the beds of the numerous soiled doves such towns attracted. It was becoming a bad habit Ezra Tindle could well do without.

But the prospector knew deep down that he would always be indebted to the young drifter. And Deakin was always quick to remind him of the fact. If it hadn't been for Curly Joe, the old dude would be stoking the fires of Hell and no mistake.

How could he ever forget. Tindle was not averse to a few noggins himself. And on one particular visit to town, he'd had special cause for celebration. His only daughter had recently qualified as a hospital nurse in St Louis, Missouri. He hadn't seen her for two years since providing the financial means of putting her through medical school. Old man Comstock had certainly done him a favour back in '59 when he'd discovered that silver lode in the eastern Sierras. The proceeds had funded her schooling.

He smiled at the recollection. And now he'd received word that she had secured a post at Sacramento's newly built hospital in California. Ezra Tindle's eyes misted over. Leaning on his shovel, he casually speculated as to how she was faring.

On his return to camp astride a less than co-operative mule, the old guy had slipped and fallen into a ravine whilst rounding the narrow trail below Angel Butte. He would have ended up as buzzard bait if young Deakin hadn't just moseyed by. Thinking back on the incident, Ezra had often wondered if the kid's sudden opportune appearance had indeed been the stroke of luck he'd figured. Or had Deakin followed him hoping for a slice of good fortune? He'd probably never know.

The old guy's dreamy ruminations were dispelled by a loud belch emanating from the confines of the lean-to.

Tindle swept the battered plainsman from his bullet head to reveal thinning grey hair. His weathered face, brown and seamed like tough saddle-leather, broke into a surly frown. He dragged a grubby red bandanna from a vest pocket and wiped the globules of sweat from his brow. Then threw down the heavy spade before stamping over to rouse the idle son-of-a-bitch.

He hadn't taken more than two steps when a vivid glint of yellow caught his eye. It came from his left behind a large rock jutting out into the creek. Another pace and it was gone. Ezra shook his head. He peered down at the swirling waters.

Nothing.

Then he stepped back a pace. There it was again.

So it hadn't been a figment of his imagination. Brilliant and crystalline, it shimmered just beneath the clear flow. His ageing heart leapt, the blood coursing through tired veins. Instantly he shrugged off weeks of accumulated lethargy. The ritual excitement that heralded a major discovery surged to the fore.

This is what it was all about. This was the dream that had spurred him on for years. And this was the obsession that had sent Ezra Tindle's wife scuttling back to the civilized trappings of St Louis along with his only child.

Barely able to contain his excitement, Ezra tentatively reached out a gnarled hand towards the gleaming object. The quivering paw hovered above the rippling surface of the creek before plunging down into its icy flow. Ezra prayed vehemently to a god he had long ignored that it was not fool's gold.

Then he had it, heavy and nobbled, rough to the touch. Reverently lifting the hunk of yellow from the creek, Ezra set it down on the sand. It was undoubtedly the biggest nugget of pure gold ever discovered in the Western Rockies. Speechless with wonder, he could only stare open-mouthed at the awesome spectacle. This was truly an historic episode. A momentous event in the annals of mining exploration.

That was the moment he realized the significance of having made such a find. The thought struck the old guy like a rampant tornado. He let out a rabid howl of delight.

'Yaaaahooo!'

Leaping to his feet with the energy of a five-year-old, he danced a spirited jig around the revered object, hallooing and yarraping for all he was worth.

Suddenly, the stained canvas awning of the lean-to swung aside and a tousled head of dark curly hair poked out. It was rapidly followed by a lanky unshaven youth of about twenty two years going on thirty. A .44 Smith & Wesson Schofield gripped in his left fist threatened a lethal termination to whomsoever had disturbed his drink-induced slumbers. Deakin had made a point of buying the pistol after learning it was the weapon favoured by his hero Jesse James.

'What's all the blamed noise about?' he yelled, loosing

off a shell into the air. The thunderous report echoing round the craggy enclave of Dirty Devil Creek quickly brought Ezra Tindle to his senses. But still he was lost for words.

'Pull yourself together, old-timer,' urged Deakin, 'and spit out what's a-buggin' you.'

Tindle could only point a gnarled talon towards the dull yellow object on the sand. Now dried off, it had lost its iridescent gleam.

Deakin frowned, imparting an ill-concealed rub of irritation. He wasn't the most patient of guys first thing.

'Don't play games, old man. I ain't in the mood for your caterwauling at this hour.'

The stark rebuff brought a steely glint to the old prospector's eye. He replaced the battered grey hat and slowly picked up the gold nugget. Squaring his sinewy frame, the old man turned towards the smirking youth.

'While you've bin sleeping it off,' he snarled, 'I've bin a graftin' for the both of us. Doin' your share of the damnblasted work.' Before Deakin could reply, Tindle thrust the object of his high spirits towards the younger man whose curiosity had been kindled. 'See what this is?' he shouted unable to contain his elation.

Deakin approached warily. Bloodshot eyes, slowly widening, were fixed on the yellow rock. He was rapidly catching on.

'You don't mean. . . .'

'Don't I just, young shaver. The biggest damn hunk of gold you ever did see.'

'And all ours.' An avaricious gleam crept into Deakin's eye. 'Lemme touch it,' he snapped making a grab for the nugget.

9

But old Ezra was too quick for him. 'Hold yer horses!' he said whipping the nugget out of reach. 'This needs sure handlin'. We don't want to bust it into a thousand pieces. As it stands, this nugget is worth a heap more than its weight in *dinero*.' Then he relented, handing the nugget to his partner with the proviso to 'treat it like you would a refined lady.'

'How much d'you reckon we'll get for it?' asked Deakin after silently stroking the fluted contours of the precious metal. His fleshy lips trembled at the thought of all the greenbacks he would soon be throwing about.

Tindle flashed him a caustic look.

'There ain't no way this lady is being cashed in just yet awhile,' he averred firmly. 'This is our insurance. This little beauty is going to be placed securely in the largest most secure bank in Colorado. And that's the Denver Central. Once it gets bandied about that the biggest gold nugget in the West is in their vaults, the value is certain to snowball.'

'What if I want the money now?' said the kid softly but with a definite hint of menace. But the intimation was lost on the old prospector. Ezra Tindle was already thinking of the fine mansion he would buy for him and his daughter in the plush new suburbs of St Louis.

'Be patient, Joe,' he replied jovially, clapping his partner on the back. 'In a year, or maybe two, you could become the wealthiest man in Colorado. If we sell it now, the gold value will be much less.'

Joe Deakin was not convinced. In fact, he was already making plans of his own for the nugget. Plans that did not involve his ageing partner. His hand visibly tightened on the black revolver, a grubby thumb stroking the hammer.

But he could wait. His time would come.

It would be another month before Tindle could make the long trip over the mountains to Denver. Winter snows blocked the high passes until mid-March so there was plenty of time. The young tearaway was equally aware that the remote location of their camp deep in the La Garita mountain fastness might well prevent him from making good his own escape south into New Mexico.

TWO

TREACHERY

Over the next two months, the heavy mantle of snow gradually slid from the endless stands of conifer trees that draped the steep valley sides of the Dirty Devil. Surrounding peaks crackled and glittered, shrugging off their icy shroud as a strengthening sun set to work. Along the creek-banks, wildlife began to appear, providing the isolated prospectors with a much welcomed supply of fresh meat, whilst spring flowers added a cheering splash of colour to the idyllic scene.

But all this was lost on Curly Joe Deakin. He was growing impatient. He was also angry that Tindle had seen fit to conceal the nugget without revealing its location. When Deakin had tackled him, the old bastard claimed it was for security reasons. But the kid knew deep down that Tindle didn't trust him. And that rankled.

Towards the end of March, Tindle announced that he would be breaking camp the following day. They had continued to work the claim, amassing a small though consistent quantity of gold dust. Enough to keep the wolf from the door according to the old prospector. Such a pronouncement raised Deakin's hackles. He had no intention of merely surviving for another two weeks, let alone two years.

That night after a rabbit supper, the young rannie made his move.

'How can I trust you not to run off with the nugget and leave me flat?' he railed, gnawing furiously on a leg.

'We've made a pact, ain't we?' responded Tindle with vigour whilst refilling his coffee mug. 'Besides, it's down in writing and signed by us both that you own half the nugget.' The old man eyed his partner quizzically.

'Pieces of paper don't mean nothing,' shot back Deakin fiercely. 'You could easily sell that gold chunk at the nearest assay office and skedaddle. And I'd be left high and dry.'

'Don't you trust me?' Tindle was visibly shocked that anyone would think him capable of such chicanery.

'Damn right I don't,' spat Deakin, jumping to his feet. His dander was well and truly up. He threw the half-chewed rabbit leg at Tindle even as he dragged the Schofield from the cross-draw holster he always favoured.

'No need for getting in such a lather, Joe,' said the old man, attempting to calm his partner down. It was clear that Deakin had been at the liquor. Bloodshot eyes were hazy with an opaque tinge, the thick voice ragged and harsh from the raw spirit. ' You can have all my gold dust if it makes you feel any better.'

'Huh!' snorted Deakin, emitting a harsh laugh that lacked any thread of humour. He shook the gun in the old man's face, snaking back the hammer. His face, gaunt and hollow, twitched with pent-up frustration. 'Think you can buy me off? No way!'

Too late the old prospector saw the glint of death in his partner's black orbs as they narrowed to deadly pin-pricks.

Without another word, Deakin pumped two rounds in quick succession into the old guy. Tindle staggered back under the impact, arms flailing wildly. He clawed desperately at the lethal punctures, blood seeping from between his fingers as he peered down, mouth agape. Slowly he raised his head, a look of utter surprise on his blanched face.

Deakin snarled, spittle edging the corners of his twisted mouth. Then he screamed, opening fire again and again, and venting all the pent-up frustration he'd built up over recent months. Tindle spun like a dancing puppet as the bullets struck home. He hit the ground with a dull thud.

Jigging around the convulsing body like some demented maniac, the young killer pumped the remaining shells into the now lifeless corpse. After another witless guffaw, he lurched away, spewing his guts up as the implication of what he had done struck home. Even though the young n'er-do-well had ridden a dicey trail since leaving home two years before, this was his first killing.

Dragging a half-empty bottle of redeye from his jacket, Deakin attempted to erase the bloody scene from his mind. Soon he was snoring, slumped in a heap beside the wasted cadaver of his erstwhile partner.

Woken next morning by a sound his drink-soused brain found difficult to fathom, Deakin struggled to prise open gritty eyes. The sight he beheld was from the bowels of Hell itself. A pair of ravenous buzzards pecking away at the bloodied corpse of Ezra Tindle. One eye hung from the optic nerve, the other had already been consumed.

Disturbed from their breakfast, the squawking duo needed no encouragement to quit the ghastly scene as Deakin lurched to his feet. As he aimed his shooter at the fleeing scavengers, the hammer clicked dully on an empty chamber.

Only then did the full meaning of his situation strike the young prospector. Any semblance of a hangover was quickly sluiced away by dousing his pounding head in the cool waters of the creek.

This was no time for regrets. What was done was done.

Now, where had the old bastard hidden the nugget?

For the rest of that day, Deakin searched everywhere within a radius of half a mile from the camp. By the time the sun was setting over the distant peaks, he was exhausted and in a foul temper. The camp was in complete disarray and he still had not located the elusive nugget.

No wonder the old bastard hadn't minded leaving him in charge of the camp while he went for supplies. He'd already secreted the treasure some place Deakin couldn't find it. The boy thumped his fist against a nearby spruce in frustration. He had killed a man and would now be a fugitive with nothing to show for it.

What a hell of a mess he'd gotten himself into!

He took a swig of whiskey to calm frayed nerves.

Now pull yourself together, Joseph Fenemore Deakin. You just sit down and think this out logically. Haven't you always managed to extricate yourself from tough scrapes in the past. Remember that whiskey drummer you robbed back in Durango. The sheriff was more than happy to believe it was those Comanches camped on the outside of town. Deakin chuckled at the recollection.

Another ample slug fired up his belly.

And those stupid geeks in Wichita Falls who'd mistaken you for their new preacher. All it needed was a few pious words and a black suit to wring a pretty handsome collection from those good folks. Gullible fools more like. Fancy figuring all those lovely greenbacks were going to build a new orphanage. Deakin's lean features broke into another perverse grin.

But this was no petty crime. We're talking murder here.

Curly Joe scratched his ample head of black hair, racking his brain for the answer.

He rolled a quirley and drew deep on the strong tobacco. A few more snorts of whiskey helped as well. Two smokes later, plus the rest of the bottle and the idea struck him with the impact of a rampaging buffalo.

This was how it would be.

Claim jumpers had heard about the gold strike and attacked at first light, killing his kind old partner and ransacking the camp. Joe would certainly have put up a spirited resistance, but he was away gathering firewood at the time and was unarmed. He had been forced to flee empty-handed, though still thankfully in one piece.

Poor old Ezra! Tears from watery eyes traced a path down his furrowed cheeks. At least Curly Joe Deakin was a good actor if nothing else.

Within the next hour the killer had packed his goods and was ready to strike camp. The half-day's journey to Telluride would give him ample chance to hone his story to perfection. When he'd finished, everybody would be eating out of his hand. Maybe things wouldn't turn out so bad after all.

After one last circuit of the old camp to make certain everything pointed to a surprise attack by unknown assailants Joey Deakin was spurring his mount back along the narrow trail. But still niggling at his warped brain was the fact that he hadn't managed to locate the biggest nugget in gold-mining history.

Finn McCall pushed the brown Texas high-crown to the back of his head allowing a thread of blond hair to snake down across his puckered forehead. Reining the mottled paint to a halt, he surveyed the bleak mountainous terrain that stretched unending to the distant horizon. A howling wind swept up from the deep ravine below Beaver Dam Pass, clamouring like a demented coyote.

The biting chill reminded Finn that winter, especially at this height, still held the land tightly in its icy grip. He pulled up his collar and hunkered down into the warmth of the thick sheepskin coat.

Tall and rangy, with a merry twinkle in his eye which reflected an easy-going nature intrinsic to his Irish ancestry, he had been born Finbar McCall twenty-eight years previously back in 1849. That was the year his father Seamus decided to escape the starvation of the Irish potato famine by seeking out a fresh start in the New World. The news of gold strikes in California had not gone unnoticed and Seamus hoped to make his pickaxe count. On the long, arduous trek west, Finn's mother had become pregnant and the family were forced to curtail their ambitions by setting down roots in the newly opened Plains territory of Kansas.

But the tough life of a sodbuster was not for Seamus McCall. And one morning when Finn could barely see above the ripening corn crop, he awoke to find himself alone with his mother. A note left by her bed stated that Seamus avowed his love for them all but would only return with his pockets stuffed full of gold nuggets. That was the last they ever heard from him.

That was until two months ago.

A dark-suited lawyer brought word to Kathy McCall that her husband had recently passed away, leaving her a chunk of fine grazing land in Western Colorado stocked with prime Hereford cattle. It appeared that Seamus had indeed struck it rich from a silver mine in Nevada.

Always the astute businessman, he had wisely invested the proceeds in the burgeoning cattle industry. And so it was that his eldest son now found himself heading west to take possession of his inheritance. He had been reluctant to leave his younger brother Patrick in charge of the farm now that his mother was not in the best of health, but knew there was no option.

'If we're plannin' to make camp for the night, best git out of this wind.'

The comment jerked Finn out of his reverie.

'How far d'you reckon we still have to go, then?' The query was aimed at Finn's stocky partner. Polecat Wilson was a good ten years older than Finn and had worked a gold claim in the territory before returning east, a totally disillusioned young man. Finn had taken him on as farm labourer and the two had become inseparable buddies.

A full head shorter than Finn, he boasted oxlike shoulders and was proportionately as strong. Polecat scratched the ragged lobe of his right ear. It was a habit that had resulted in the odd name with which he had reluctantly been saddled.

One night after supper on his gold claim, Jimmy Wilson had been cleaning the bacon grease from his frying-pan. He had then unwittingly scratched his ear before falling asleep aided by a liberal supply of home-brewed snake-eye. A nocturnal visitor of the four-legged variety had chewed off half the exposed appendage, much to Wilson's consternation the next morning.

Unlike Wilson, the local sawbones found the story hilarious and it soon spread like wildfire throughout the goldfields. From that day forward, Jimmy Wilson would be forever known as *Polecat*.

He stepped down from the red mustang. Again scratching at his ragged ear, Polecat stretched his arms to ease tired muscles. Fiery locks complementing the deep-red sandstone crags of the pass floated free as he lifted a stiff-brimmed Montana high-peak. Deep set eyes picked out the distant horizon against the azure backdrop of a westering sun.

'I figure two days should bring us to Telluride,' he replied after due consideration. He replaced the hat, rolled a quirley and fired up. Blue smoke twisted and writhed in the stiff breeze.

'What sort of place is Telluride?' Finn asked, eager to discover more about this land with which he had suddenly become involved.

'A bit of a rough and ready town. It blew up with the speed of a Utah sandstorm when gold fever hit the territory in sixty-eight,' elucidated Polecat, chewing on a strip of beef jerky. 'A one-horse town just like a thousand others littering the West. Soon as the gold fades, so will the town.' A flight of meadowlarks swooped low over the tops of a nearby stand of pine. Late snows to the north impinged on Polecat's thoughts.

'Yup!' he nodded sagely, stroking his stubbly chin. 'Two days should do it. Then another five down the Gunnison.' A hesitant pause followed. 'That is if we take the San Miguel cut-off.'

'Let's hope we don't get ourselves bogged down in a rogue snowfall,' added Finn, fastening his keen gaze on them pesky grey cloud bolls that persistently nudged the jagged peaks. He gratefully accepted a roll-up from his partner and sat down on a rock, studying the narrow trail that fell away steeply into the valley bottom. It was soon lost amidst the sylvan blanket of dense pine cloaking the slopes below the pass.

Following the brief respite, they gingerly eased their mounts warily down the track. Isolated banks of snow made for a precarious descent to valley level. More than once the pair were almost unseated when iron-shod hoofs failed to grip the slippery terrain.

THREE

TELLURIDE

By the time Curly Joe Deakin reached the outskirts of Telluride, he had his story word perfect. The sheriff was the man who had to be won over. A sidekick of his ex-partner's from way back, the two had ridden together for a spell during the Nevada silver strike of 1860.

He cast a wary eye over the untidy huddle of buildings.

A loose collection of clapboard hovels and grubby lean-tos lined the main drag. Few had witnessed a lick of paint. Much of the bare wood had warped and was rotting from exposure to the elements. Sawn-off tree-stumps littered both sides of the valley, the timber having been commandeered for pit props as well as for the town itself. An odd tree here and there had been left, the only concession made to embellishing the place. But overall the appearance of Telluride was one of utter despoliation. Concern for the environment was the last thing on anybody's mind here.

Gold was king. And Telluride, like many of its contem-

21

poraries, was not intended as a place to cure depression.

As the snows had thawed, so the roadway had been churned into an ocean of mud. Deakin nudged his mount down the edge to avoid the worst of the sludge. His objective was half way down on the right. The sheriff's office was the only stone-built structure in Telluride. Though even that was a false image of solidity, the rest of the building being made from hard-packed adobe.

Deakin tethered his horse to the hitching post, stepped on to the boardwalk and paused. Furtively he peered up and down the grim street. Nobody paid him any heed. Just another prospector down on his luck.

Hat pushed askew, neckerchief all ragged, Deakin squared his narrow shoulders. Swallowing hard he lumbered straight in through the thick oak door without knocking. It slammed back against the wall, rattling the window-frame.

A short grizzled man of indeterminate vintage was over by the stove pouring a cup of coffee from a large blackened pot. His thick grey moustache bristled indignantly.

'What's all this?' he snapped, spilling the hot liquid on the floor. 'You cain't come bargin' in here like some loco mule.' He had clearly taken umbrage at having his lunchtime break disturbed.

Jake Montane was the wrong side of fifty. Stooped shoulders testified to a lifetime of humping gold tailings. He'd taken the job of sheriff thinking it would be an easier way of spending his latter years than fruitlessly scrabbling about in creek-beds for what little gold remained in this part of Colorado. All his life, Jake had dreamed of striking it rich, only to end up flat broke in this two-bit shanty town.

Stubborn and crotchety, he slammed the pot down and faced the intruder. A wary eye poked from beneath unkempt brows, his gnarled right hand resting on the Army Remington at his hip.

On more than one occasion he had refused to be browbeaten by claim jumpers; his trusty twelve-gauge sending 'em packing with a flea in their ear. Montane was no slouch when it came to gunplay. But he lacked the draw-speed of his youth and had discovered that a more thoughtful approach, approximating to guile and cunning, was the key to a long life. Too many of his contemporaries had run into desperadoes just that touch faster. Now they were permanent residents on Boot Hill.

More often than not in the past it was the brash show-offs who had won the coveted jobs of town lawdog. So Jake had not hesitated, even though taken by surprise, when the town council had offered him a job nobody else wanted.

Forty a month and found was not to be sniffed at by an old-timer in his position. So he'd pinned on the tin star. And it felt good. For the first time in his life Jake Montane was respected. An upright citizen.

So he expected a little civility when folks came asking for his help.

Deakin staggered to a halt in the middle of the small outer office of the jail. His shoulders heaved, breath coming in short laboured gasps.

'Cat gotten yer tongue, mister?' enquired the sheriff, screwing up his already rumpled visage. The surprise visitor was clearly not after busting his prisoner out of the hoosegow. Not that anybody would have a notion to free Jackdaw Lassiter. If anyone could make a profession out of scrounging drinks, it was Lassiter, a regular patron of the jail's cell-block.

Deakin slumped into a chair, giving the impression of a man in dire straits. He dragged the crumpled hat from his mop of curly hair and wiped a creased forehead with the loose necker.

The sheriff waited, impatience etched across his furrowed brow.

Then it all came out.

'Me and my partner was jumped,' Deakin wheezed, injecting every last morsel of dramatic flair into the act. 'They surprised us at sun-up. Lucky for me I was up gathering wood for the fire else I'd have ended up like poor old Ezra.' He paused for effect. Thin lips puckered to complement the hangdog expression.

Montane urged him on. 'What happened to him?'

'Gunned down in cold blood when he wouldn't disclose where he'd hidden the loot.'

'And you let them varmints get away with murdering your partner?' Montane eyed the younger man sceptically. Ezra Tindle was (or had been) well known in this part of Colorado. A character like many of his breed. And much liked.

'What could I do?' pleaded Deakin jumping to his feet and gesticulating wildly. 'I was unarmed. I'd have ended up buzzard bait for no reason.'

The sheriff pulled at his moustache, a quizzical expression crossing his seamed face. He'd had to deal with a couple of claim-jumpers since he'd become sheriff three months before. But neither had led to a killing.

'How many was there?' he enquired.

'Two, maybe three.'

'Can you describe them?'

'Ornery-looking fellas. Nothing special. I kept my head down when the gunplay started.'

'What did they say? Any names mentioned?'

'Can't recall anythin'.'

Deakin was beginning to feel a mite flustered. Beads of sweat trickled down his forehead. He quickly wiped them away. He hadn't figured on being interrogated like this. The sheriff was asking too many damn fool questions.

'Anyhow, oughtn't you best be fixing up a posse to ride out there?' he challenged. The belligerent tone was intended to show that such action was the obvious course to be taken.

'Not so fast there,' quieted Montane, moving over to refill his coffee mug. 'This needs thinkin' on. No sense in rushing out to Dirty Devil Creek now. The deed's bin done.'

'Maybe so. But every minute wasted around here is letting them dry-gulchers escape.'

'Hmmm!' Montane had never been one to rush into things half-cocked. He took another sip of his coffee. Then he fired up a smoke. Blue tendrils drifted from the corner of his mouth, watery eyes pursuing the snaky threads.

Jake Montane was thinking. A process that had served him well in the past.

Deakin eyeballed him warily, trying to judge the lawdog's stance on the matter. He didn't have long to wait.

Without uttering another word, the sheriff made for the still-open door. He grabbed an old tan plainsman from its peg and slammed it on his balding pate, then checked the load of a well-oiled twelve-bore. Deakin followed him out on to the boardwalk.

Almost as an afterthought Montane added, 'Be outside the Silver Dollar in thirty minutes. Tooled up and ready to ride.'

'You want me along?'

Surprise was etched across Deakin's clouded brow. This was not part of the plan. He had hoped to catch up on lost drinking time. That gold dust he'd amassed might not be a king's ransom, but it was sure burning a hole in his pocket. The last place he wanted to be was the scene of his recent débâcle.

The sheriff screwed up his wizened visage.

'What d'you expect?' he growled, throwing a leery glance at the youngster. 'You're the prime witness. And anyways, I need you to guide us there. Ain't never passed through the Dirty Devil afore.' The older man fixed Deakin with a baleful glare. 'You got a problem with that?'

Not wishing to encourage any doubts as to the reality of his story, Deakin quickly stifled his fears.

'Sure thing, Sheriff. Anything you say. I just wanna find the crawling scum what shot my partner.'

Montane gave a shrug, then stumped off along the boardwalk in search of likely volunteers for a posse. Not always an easy task, as he'd found on previous occasions when desperadoes needed hunting down.

There was never a problem when a high reward was offered, but a random incident like the present case when the town's leading citizens were not involved was another matter entirely. Two hours later, Curly Joe was still propping up the bar of the Silver Dollar when the sheriff called to him from the doorway.

'You ready then, feller?' he asked.

'Have been for a coon's age,' grumbled the kid, swilling down the last dregs of his beer. Wiping a sleeve across thin lips, he followed the lawman outside and surveyed the motley crew with scornful disdain.

'Call this a posse?' he smirked. Not that it mattered who came just so long as this damn lawdog believed his story. That was what mattered. Deakin unhitched his mount and climbed into the saddle. The meagre posse headed out of town behind the sheriff; Deakin followed closely by Jackdaw Lassiter and a couple of panners down on their luck.

Montane had managed to persuade the town council to put up a reward for the apprehension of the miscreants. But they would only go to one hundred dollars.

'A measly one hundred bucks!' scoffed Deakin when he was informed.

'Don't blame me,' responded the sheriff vehemently. 'He was my friend too.'

'So these three layabouts were all you could muster,' snapped Deakin. His response was heavy with unsuppressed sarcasm. 'That much'll keep us in whiskey for all of what – two days?'

The kid was really into his stride. He'd almost forgotten it was he whom the posse was after. And all he was worth amounted to a paltry one hundred dollars.

He grunted derisively.

'Something bothering you, kid?' snapped Montane, glaring testily. This kid was rapidly eating into his craw.

The sheriff's petulance was a jolting reminder for him to cool it.

'Just thinking that poor old Ezra was worth a heap

more'n a hundred dollars,' countered Deakin, quickly spurring his horse down the main street ahead of the others.

Heading east, the small party soon began to climb out of the broad park of the San Juan. The trail meandered between sparse remnants of ravaged pine stands. Once they were above the steep lower slopes and riding across the higher plateau, Telluride appeared as no more than a grey smudge staining the bottomland. Eastward, a clear trail wide enough for mine wagons ran straight as a Comanche lance to the distant horizon of the La Garitas. Beyond the workings of War Bonnet Mine, it faded to a narrow track along the base of the soaring mesa known as Stanton's Bluff.

Deakin shrugged deeper into his sheepskin as the colder air nipped at his vitals. Towards late afternoon the small group of riders were passing the grandiose upthrust of Chimney Rock. A noted landmark visible for miles, the multilayered sandstone monolith stood proud and defiant: a steadfast sentinel guarding the entrance to the Dirty Devil. For the rest of the journey, they would be forced to ride in single file between dense ranks of pine that flourished in the claustrophobic atmosphere.

It would be another hour before they reached the camp. The abrupt realization brought a lump to Deakin's throat. He would have to keep his wits about him from here on.

FOUR

ARREST

It was late afternoon the following day when Finn raised his right hand to signal a halt. They had just rounded a promontory thrusting out into Dirty Devil Creek adjoining the tortuous trail. He pointed towards a canvas lean-to slung between a couple of pine trunks on the far side of the swirling water. It was their first sign of human life since trailing out of Concord four days previously.

It certainly gave the appearance of being a campsite. But there was nobody around. And it sure looked a mess even when viewed from aways off. Gear and supplies were scattered across the creek terrace in wanton profusion.

He was about to call out when Polecat grabbed his arm.

'No point announcing our presence just yet awhile,' he whispered. 'Looks like a miners' camp. And them fellers are like as not to haul iron and blast us if'n they feel threatened.'

'What d'you suggest?'

Although acknowledged as the boss, Finn had never

29

been too proud or arrogant when it came to heeding the advice of those with more experience, be it choice of seed, use of artificial fertilizer, or how to approach a potentially hostile situation.

'Let's hold off a spell and see what happens.'

For thirty minutes they studied the camp. Watching, waiting, scanning the adjoining terrain for any suspicious movement.

There was none. The place had clearly been abandoned.

Polecat edged forward. He hauled out a Henry carbine from its leather scabbard, levered a shell into the breech, then kept a finger poised on the trigger guard.

As they came nearer to the camp it quickly became apparent that a violent fracas had taken place.

Finn quit his saddle and carefully approached the still body of Ezra Tindle. It was lying at an ungainly angle, face down in a pool of dried blood. He levered the body on to its back with his boot; the gory mess of a head pecked clean made his stomach lurch. As if to remind him of the precarious nature of surviving in the wilderness, a lone buzzard floated by overhead. It squawked derisively.

'Looks to me like a disagreement over the share-out led to terminal gunplay,' croaked Polecat.

'And this guy lost the argument,' added Finn, his nose wrinkling with distaste. He quickly turned away to search the rest of the camp. 'The place has been completely plundered,' he remarked with a knowing frown. 'Everything's either broken or strewn about.'

'Could be that the killer was looking for something,' Polecat mused thoughtfully, slinging a thumb at the recumbent form, which had attracted a host of flies.

'Probably that dude's hidden poke. Even lifelong buddies get to bein' suspicious of each other where gold's concerned.'

Lengthening shadows crept silently across the creek bottom as the sun slipped below the jagged rimrock. The turgid green of endless pine blurred to a dusky opacity, a reminder that nightfall would soon be upon them.

'Better make camp here for the night,' suggested Polecat. 'We can make use of the abandoned gear.'

'I'll gather up some wood,' said Finn, eyeing the grotesque body, 'and set up over there.' He nodded to a piece of flat ground as far away from the bloodied corpse as possible.

In no time, a fire was crackling and the bacon sizzling.

It was the smell that first alerted Jake Montane. No mistaking that distinct aroma, which could mean only one thing. They were not alone.

Jackdaw Lassiter was the first to spot the tendrils of smoke drifting above the pine tops. He pointed a knotty finger.

'Seems like some critter got here afore us,' he commented acidly.

Deakin's heart missed a beat. For an instant his blood ran cold. An icy tremor launched itself down his spine. Surely the old bastard couldn't still be alive.

Never. Not after all that lead he'd taken.

So if it wasn't Ezra Tindle, who the hell. . . ?

Montane signalled a halt: a single finger raised to pursed lips, indicating silence. Carefully the posse dismounted and checked their guns. The two panners, twins going by the names of Amos and Caleb Flagg,

31

sported an ancient Dragoon apiece. Heavy and cumbersome, the barrels were pitted with rust. Fearsome weapons in their day, by 1877 they were outmoded and old-fashioned.

Deakin scoffed. His contempt for the two prospectors was blatant and challenging.

Deftly, he flipped the hammer of his gleaming Schofield to half-cock and spun the chamber. The blued metal glinted in the rays from the setting sun. Normally only five cylinders were loaded, for safety while riding. He now pressed a final shell into the empty pod and slammed the chambers shut.

A final spin of the revolver for effect completed the flamboyant display.

'Now that's what I call a real piece of hardware,' he smirked, twirling the hogleg on his middle finger in the manner of the Denver roll before sliding it back into the oiled holster.

An irate growl fizzed from between Caleb Flagg's thin lips. His hand strayed to the large revolver on his hip. His more circumspect brother quickly pushed himself between Caleb and the young hothead, a timely reminder that the pair of miners were no gunfighters. Their time would come.

Montane also sensed the brewing tension and quickly brought Deakin back to the reality of their situation.

'That thing ain't just for show, is it, mister?' he jeered with an astute wink at the others. 'Looks like you might have to use it pretty soon – if'n you got the bottle, that is.'

Deakin shot him a venomous glare.

'What we waitin' fer then,' he snarled, squaring his broad shoulders. 'Independence Day?' Turning on his heel, the kid stumped off towards the rising plume of smoke.

'Easy there, kid,' hissed the sheriff. 'This needs careful handlin' if we aim to do the job properly.' Hefting the trusty twelve-gauge, he checked the twin barrels were loaded, then pocketed a handful of spare cartridges. His next remark was aimed at them all.

'Spread out and watch your footing,' he counselled. 'A broken twig is all it needs to set the cat among the pigeons.'

'Lookee what we have here, Polecat.'

The older man flicked the bacon over in the frying pan before glancing across at what his partner was holding aloft.

'Tinned peaches.' Finn's mouth watered in anticipation. 'Ain't tasted these since before the fall. Remember that visit to Clarksville?'

Polecat nodded, equally tempted by the succulent allure of the yellow fruit.

But he was given no opportunity to reply.

In the flick of a rattler's tongue, a .44 shell slammed into the frying-pan, sending the contents spewing in all directions. The shock at this violent interruption to his supper sent the redhead tumbling back, legs all a-tangle. Swiftly recovering from the stunned jolt, he scrambled across the open ground crablike to reach his rifle.

He never made it.

The next shot thudded into his back. Arching fiercely under the brutal impact, his spine disintegrated. Polecat's mouth flapped soundlessly like a stranded pike, his quivering hand desperately reaching for the weapon.

Another blast cut short the futile efforts. His smashed body shuddered violently, obscenely jerking, then lay still.

The lethal weapon swung with potent menace to cover Finn McCall.

'Make one wrong move, pilgrim,' rasped Deakin, his voice strained and gravelly, 'and you'll be heading down the glory road alongside this dude.' The Schofield waved and floated in front of Finn's staring optics, rooting him to the spot. Aghast, horrified, he was unable to comprehend the violent course events had suddenly taken.

Slowly he shifted his bewildered gaze to the shattered body of his friend and partner.

It was then that the other members of the unlikely posse hustled into the clearing, guns drawn and ready for use.

'What happened here?' barked the sheriff.

'This turkey,' replied Deakin indicating the sprawled heap that had been Polecat Wilson, 'went for his gun. I had no choice but to cut loose. It was him or me.' He shrugged, nonchalently blowing smoke from the end of his pistol. 'No contest.'

Curly Joe Deakin displayed an evil grin. He was rapidly acquiring a taste for gunplay of the terminal variety.

Montane grunted but hadn't failed to note the unashamed grimace souring the other man's face.

The next remark was aimed at the bewildered young man.

'Seems like you've been caught out red-handed, mister,' snarled Amos Flagg, jabbing his heavy pistol at the cowering farmer. 'We don't take kindly to murdering claim-jumpers in these parts.'

The others grunted in agreement, pressing forward ominously.

Jackdaw Lassiter pushed the young farmer in the back sending him sprawling into the open. An ugly scowl split his soused features.

Finn was quickly surrounded. Five loaded gun barrels threatened to blast him into the next state at any minute. Not to mention that deadly piece of hemp swaying back and forth in Lassiter's hand. It was this realization that brought the young farmer to his senses. That and the rancid odour from stale liquor and unwashed bodies crowding in on him.

Still clutching hold of the peaches, he lurched backwards, hurling the heavy tin at the hostile posse. It struck Caleb Flagg a resounding thwack on the knee.

'Yikes!' howled the miner, hopping about on his uninjured leg.

Ignoring the shrill yelps of pain, Deakin sensed an opportunity to finish matters quickly.

'Let's string him up to the nearest tree,' he hollered, making to grab Finn's hair. The last thing he wanted was this rannie putting doubts in the mind of the sheriff. 'Gimme that rope, Jackdaw,' he snapped.

Before the town drunk could move, the sheriff hauled him short.

'There'll be no lynchings while I'm in charge.' His tone was measured and even but with clear intent. A knotty hand gently caressed the polished rosewood stock of the shotgun. In his grey eyes, a flinty gleam challenged anybody to defy his authority. Nobody did.

Turning to Finn he asked bluntly, 'So what you gotta say 'bout what's happened here?'

Fully recovered from the initial shock and thankful for the lawman's intercession, Finn vehemently protested his innocence.

'The old guy was dead when we arrived,' he averred fervently, gesticulating with both hands. 'Somebody must have plugged him then ransacked the camp to find his gold.'

His reasoning met with a stony silence. Scepticism, cold and merciless, was clearly etched on each man's features. The hunched guy referred to as Jackdaw ominously twirled the saddle rope in his gnarled hands.

Only the sheriff could be relied on to maintain the rule of law in this remote wilderness.

'It's God's own truth, mister,' pleaded Finn, his cracked voice dry and husky with trepidation. 'We were heading for the San Juan country to take over a ranch. This is none of our doing. I swear it. We just happened along by accident.' But there was a tight lump in his guts telling him that his appeal to reason had fallen on stony ground.

The highly charged atmosphere in the small basin simmered with menace. Time stood still, the tense posse facing off the accused man. A heavy silence, brief and poignant, drew down on the clearing. Grey skeins of mist rose from the chattering creek as the sun tipped below the watching pine stands.

'Yeh!' sneered Deakin eventually, 'And the moon's made of green cheese. An innocent man don't resist when challenged.' He nodded towards Wilson's recumbent body.

Montane gave a curt shrug of indifference.

Finn prayed the lawman would not give in and let the others have their way. It had happened many times before.

Vigilante law in far-flung outposts of the frontier was a common enough fact of life. Miners' courts didn't go much on evidence. And many a wronged man had found himself the star guest at a necktie party.

Finn's very existence now hung in the balance.

Obviously, none of the posse believed a word of his story.

'I still say we stretch his neck here and now,' repeated Deakin, urging the others to take the law into their own hands. 'It'll save the town the expense of a trial.'

'That's right! String the murdering bastard up,' echoed both Flagg brothers in unison.

Sensing an animal blood lust about to take control, Montane hefted the shotgun and let rip with one of barrels into the air. The timely blast immediately cut short the guttural cries for retribution.

His steely gaze surveyed the gathering.

'I'm the only law round here. And that's official now that Colorado's been granted statehood. No more mob rule or vigilante tribunals. Them days is plumb over and done with.' The sway of the lethal smoking gun, like a vexed sidewinder, effectively backed up his claim. Montane paused, stubbly chin jutting forward, as if goading the others to defy his authority. 'This man goes back to Telluride to stand trial the next time the circuit judge comes a-visitin'.' Then for Deakin's benefit. 'In my jurisdiction, the law *will* be upheld.'

Not waiting for any dissent, he ordered Lassiter to tether the prisoner to a nearby tree. Deep shadows, thick and heavy, had settled over the clearing heralding the imminent approach of darkness. They had little option but to spend the night in this ghoulish spot and return to

Telluride on the morrow.

But first there were two graves to be dug. After setting the Flagg twins to work, the sheriff sauntered over to ensure that Lassiter had adequately secured his prisoner.

Finn sighed audibly. 'Much obliged for your intervention, Sheriff,' he said.

The older man laid a hawkish eye on him. Then nodded his acknowledgement.

'Mister,' he spoke firmly, emphasizing each word, 'I'll make damn sure you'll be gettin' a fair trial when I git you back to Telluride. Nobody's about to take the law into their own hands in my territory.' A sly crease, neither a smile nor a sneer, broke across the sheriff's usually impassive features, revealing an uneven set of teeth, much yellowed by constant baccy chewing. A brown stream of juice flicked from the corner of his mouth.

His final rejoinder before sidling off did nothing to raise the prisoner's hopes that a bright future lay ahead.

'*Then* I'll hang you!'

FIVE

PURSUIT

Early the next morning, the posse and its reluctant guest were soon on the trail heading back to Telluride. The sheriff rode at the rear of the column to forestall the unlikely event of any of these jaspers deciding to obstruct the due process of the law. That hothead Curly Joe Deakin needed special watching. Definitely something mean and vicious about him – too friggin' quick at pointing the finger.

By midday, with a weak sun struggling to push aside the grey mantle hanging low over the La Garitas, the small posse had come in sight of the untidy clutter that was Telluride. Occasional glimpses of blue poking through from above added a splash of colour to an otherwise drab scene. Not that anybody gave a donkey's fart. This was gold-mining country – pure and simple.

Trundling down the main street the small party, complete with their prisoner, attracted a host of curious onlookers. Someone else's misfortune always provoked interest. It livened up the dull existence of life in such places. And they all knew what this was about. News about claim-jumpers always spreads like wildfire in gold camps.

'Caught the bastard what done fer old Ezra then, Sheriff?' enquired a gruff voice from amidst the gathering throng.

'No need fer a trial then,' shouted another, articulating the growing mood of the bystanders.

'String him up!'

Montane stiffened. He raised the shotgun, swinging it round menacingly.

'First man that makes a move in that direction'll git both barrels in the gut.'

His tone, gritty and brooking no dispute, quelled the threatening temper of the mob. Not waiting to test their resolve, he hurriedly pushed on down the street followed at some distance by the murmuring crowd.

Once inside the hoosegow, the prisoner was quickly locked up in one of the grubby cells at the rear of the building. It smelt as bad as it looked. A variety of lurid comments carved by past detainees littered the rough-cast adobe walls.

Finn peered around at his bleak surroundings. A heavy sense of impending doom settled over his bent shoulders. Was this how he was going to end his days? Waiting for some judge to pass the ultimate sentence, then feeling the rough hemp choking his life away.

It took all the young man's determination to prevent himself breaking down. Some time later, a scraping of boot heels broke in on his morbid reflections as the sheriff came through from the front office. He was carrying a tray covered with a red-checked cloth. Even through the murky depths of Finn's distraught ruminations, the food smelt good.

'Best enjoy this while you can, mister,' said the old tin star, pushing the tray through a gap at the base of the iron-barred door. Then he added, 'I'll make sure you enjoy the full protection of the law . . . for as long as you're my house guest.' Montane couldn't help smiling at his astute turn of phrase. 'Yes sir. Can't have the mob doin' me out of a job now, can we?'

'When will the judge arrive?' asked Finn, ignoring the jibe.

The sheriff scratched his greying thatch.

'Hummm!' he mused. 'Reckon about two weeks should see Old Black Towel setting up shop over in the saloon.'

Finn eyed him, a puzzled frown creasing his forehead.

'Zebediah Took,' offered Montane in answer to his unspoken query. 'Best judge in the territory. He always wears a black square of cloth on his head just before passing sentence. Fer a hangin' that is,' he added as an afterthought. 'Seems like he picked up the habit from some relation of his who sits on the bench back in the old country.' Without further explanation the sheriff turned away. 'Enjoy the meal,' he said brightly, 'You're a lucky fella. Josie Green from the Pancake House across the street is the finest cook in these parts.'

Finn's appetite had suddenly deserted him. The appetizing food forgotten, he flopped down staring blankly at the uneven brown wall. A lark bunting perched cheekily on the edge of the barred window, its plump body etched starkly against the grey backdrop outside. Chirpily, it regarded the captive. Never had the young man envied the freedom of this tiny creature more. Then it was gone.

A brisk flap of dark feathers and Finn was left alone to review his sorry plight.

'Why ain't we heard from Finn?'

The question posed by Patrick McCall was aimed at a tall statuesque woman with long blond hair tied back with a green velvet ribbon. The pair were in the outhouse cleaning harness and tack ready for the spring seed planting. Daisy, their old plough mare, munched lazily at her feed trough. 'He's bin gone more 'n a month now.' The worry was clearly evident in the harsh timbre of the lad's voice.

'Now don't you fret none,' replied his mother quietly. 'It'll have been plumb nigh impossible to get any message back here this quick.' Even though she was mightily concerned about the whereabouts of her eldest son, coolness under pressure had always been a feature of her personality. It had seen the family through hard times since her husband had upped stakes and disappeared. 'Be patient,' she urged.

But her younger son was anything but composed. Unlike his brother, Paddy McCall had always been volatile and quick of temper. It had gotten him into more scrapes than he could remember at school. Now that he was approaching manhood, Katy had the devil of a job keeping the young feller under control.

And recently, he had acquired one of them six-shooters everybody was talking about – the Colt Peacemaker. Only the other day she had found him behind the barn practising how to draw and fire from the hip. Kate knew that was the way of the gunfighter and she was exceedingly concerned that the boy would land himself in deep trouble.

42

'You know what Finn's been like since Pa left,' continued Paddy failing to sense his mother's alarm. 'Always insisted I keep in touch even if it was only for one night. So he'd have been sure to send word about where he was by now.'

Still Kate McCall tried to evade the reality of the situation. Methodically she unravelled a set of leather reins, dusty and tough from lack of use over the winter months.

'Don't mean he's in trouble,' she alleged somewhat lamely.

'Well I figure he is,' countered her son with conviction. He threw down a set of brasses he was polishing. They clanged ominously on the hard-packed dirt floor. 'He would have sent a wire to the telegraph office in town.'

Plaintree was the nearest town of any size. Paddy had ridden there only the day before for that express purpose.

Not a word.

That had settled the issue in his mind. His brother was in trouble.

Shoulders set, a steely glint in his eye, Paddy went out to the corral to saddle his horse, a chestnut mare going by the name of Spike.

'What you doing, son?' she called after him. But already he had disappeared into the house. Ten minutes later the young man emerged toting a bed roll under his left arm and clutching a set of worn saddle-bags stuffed with supplies. Enough for a week's travel. After that he was in God's hands.

His distraught mother begged him not to be hasty. But the kid's mind was made up. At last, perceiving her grave apprehension and fear, Paddy quietly strove to reassure her.

'Don't you be worrying yourself, Ma. I'll be fine. Ain't I the best shot with a long rifle in the county?' He patted the ancient single-shot Hawken.

'That's what worries me,' croaked his mother. A single teardrop traced a path down her drawn features. She dabbed at it with the hem of her apron. 'You might get yourself killed. Then where would I be? First your father, then Finbar. And now you.' The distressed woman could no longer hold back the flood of tears.

'Now then, Ma. You know I don't have any choice.' He took his mother in his arms and comforted her shuddering frame. But his tanned features betrayed a rigid determination. There was no going back now. 'No choice,' he repeated quietly. 'And anyways,' he added after extricating himself from the maternal clutches, 'the Millers will see you come to no harm. I'll call at their farm and put 'em in the picture.'

Persuading his mother that there was no alternative took all Paddy's diplomatic acumen. Not something he readily undertook. Not until after midday was he at last able to make his farewells.

The last view Kate McCall had of her younger son was of him waving the old Hawken. Then he was gone, out of sight, heading west for Colorado on the trail of his elder brother.

SIX

CONSPIRACY

Jake Montane was doing his morning rounds. Ambling down the main street of Telluride, he struggled unsuccessfully to avoid the worst of the mud. His boots were caked in a thick glutinous ooze as he mounted the boardwalk adjoining the Silver Dollar saloon. Looking in through the front window he could see that even at this early hour the place was doing a brisk trade. A shambling form hustling through the batwings almost collided with him.

'Where are you rushin' off to in such an all-fired hurry?' asked the sheriff, placing a firm hand on the man's chest. Montane backed off instinctively as a repulsive mixture of sweat, stale booze and vomit assailed his senses.

Curly Joe Deakin looked a pitiful sight. His clothes were untidy and dishevelled, his normally handsome features were haggard and unshaven. Not a trace of the cocky young rannigan whose vital testimony had convicted the claim-jumper two weeks before. Montane repeated his question, regarding the odious creature evenly.

Deakin returned his gaze. Then curled his lip.

'I figure you owe me, Sheriff,' he hissed, clutching at the saloon doorjamb. He was clearly the worse for drink.

'Go sleep it off, feller,' responded Montane ignoring the remark. 'We'll talk later.'

Attempting to push past, Deakin grabbed at his arm.

'I said you owe me.' The swaying drunk refused to be deterred. 'That reward is mine. I earned it fair and square. An' now that the killer's waitin' on his due, I want payin' off.'

Hearing the commotion outside, a few of the saloon's regular patrons had gathered at the open doorway. The jangling piano had ceased its cacophony.

'So what you gonna do 'bout it?' snarled Deakin, drawing encouragement from his audience. 'Do I git paid? Or—'

'Or what, mister?' Montane interrupted, drawing his Remington. He jabbed the cold metal of the barrel up the kid's reddening snout.

Gasps issued from the gathering crowd, all hoping for some action. Deakin's bloodshot eyes widened. The soporific effects of the booze were rapidly evaporating.

'No cause for any gunplay, Sheriff,' he said in an aggrieved tone. 'Just want what I'm due. That's all.'

Montane considered, then responded sharply:

'I'll be meetin' with the town council at noon. Come by the office around five this evening and you kin have yer blood-money.'

With that he stamped off, slamming the pistol back into its holster.

'Good on you, Joe,' called out one bystander.

'That showed the pesky lawdog,' from another.

'Let me buy you a drink,' offered a third, slapping him on the back.

They all shouldered back through the doors and made for the long bar. Immediately, the yammering clank of the piano recommenced. It was accompanied by the tuneless voice of a gaudily painted songstress who passionately strove to replicate the words of a popular ditty. Her thickly rouged lips leered at Deakin.

The soused kid was slow to realize that any jasper coming into money always attracts a glut of new buddies. And now that his poke of the yellow stuff had disappeared over the shiny bar top of the Silver Dollar, the kid desperately needed that reward.

But not all the occupants of the smoky saloon were as enthusiastic. In a corner, huddled over a bottle of cheap redeye, three men muttered and glowered. Jackdaw Lassiter grabbed the half-empty bottle from Amos Flagg. After all, he'd worked for it, swabbing out the grubby floor of the saloon that morning.

'That bastard oughta be sharin' the reward with us,' he grumbled, coughing as the rotgut whiskey burned a hole in his stomach. He hawked a gob of phlegm into a nearby spittoon. His aim was spot on from years of practice.

Sitting opposite, Caleb Flagg idly carved a cross into the pinewood table with his Bowie knife. It was the nearest he would ever come to signing his name. Unlike his brother, who was the elder by twenty minutes, the lumbering ox of a miner was no scholar. Amos did all the thinking for them both. Caleb just provided the muscle.

He pointed the wicked tip of the knife at Deakin's back.

'Seems to me like we oughta do somethin' about it,' he

said snatching at the bottle.

Lassiter growled, but said nothing.

'Could be you're right about that, Caleb,' nodded his brother. 'Though I wasn't thinkin' on no share-out.'

The scheming trio huddled closer. Following a whispered conflab, an observant patron might have noticed three evil grins spearing the unsuspecting back of the young killer.

It was early evening. Light cast by the numerous establishments reflected from muddy puddles on the street. Thankfully it had stopped raining. Just a steady drip, drip, drip from the overhangs accompanied Deakin back to the Silver Dollar. Grudgingly, the sheriff had paid out and the young rannie now had one hundred greenbacks stuffed into his pockets.

A sickly grin of anticipation split his coarsened face.

At that hour, the saloon was empty. All the usual patrons had retired to their tents, lodgings or flophouses to recoup sapped energy. The coming night's party with Curly Joe Deakin as guest of honour promised to be a right wingdinger.

That suited the two conspirators perfectly. But where was Jackdaw Lassiter? The idle bum was supposed to have met the Flagg twins at five sharp behind the saloon. He was not there.

'Where's that lazy bastard got to?' hissed Amos Flagg. Caleb merely shrugged his huge shoulders. That was when they heard a low rumble coming from inside the storeroom at the rear of the saloon. Amos whipped out his pistol.

'What was that?'

'Sounds like a mountain lion to me,' muttered Caleb.

'In town, you dumb ox?' snorted Amos derisively, shaking his head.

'I wus only tryin' to help,' whined the big man oafishly.

'Well don't. I'll do the thinkin' for the both of us.' Amos gave his brother a withering glare. 'Right?'

'Sure, sure thing, Amos.'

'Well then, gimme some room.' Amos Flagg shouldered his brother out of the way and peered in through the dirt-encrusted window. His uncouth features hardened into an angry snarl.

'What is it?' asked Caleb pushing forward.

Ignoring the question, Amos quietly opened the door and stepped into the gloomy interior. It was full of beer barrels, crates of wine and bags of sawdust. These last were used to soak up spilt liquor on the saloon floor. And propped up against one of them with an empty wine bottle in his hand was Jackdaw Lassiter. Dead to the world, a hoarse rumble emanated from his dry throat.

Amos bent down, grabbed a handful of shirt collar and shook him roughly, at the same time delivering a stinging blow to the side of the head.

'Wake up, you drunken turd,' he growled. 'We got work to do.'

The only response was a choking gurgle. Amos threw the dead weight back against the sack. Caleb made his own contribution to rousing the recumbent form by aiming a savage kick to his ribs. Even that failed to elicit more than a stifled groan.

Then Amos smiled wolfishly. An idea had struck his warped brain.

'This means there's only the two of us sharin' the reward money.'

'What'll I git then?' bleated Caleb.

'Same as always,' smirked Amos. But his brother had failed to perceive the sly gleam in his hooded eye. 'We split it right down the middle. That means out of a one-hundred-dollar reward, you get forty.' Amos glanced at his brother. 'That suit you?'

Caleb's fleshy mouth creased as he gave a couple of satisfied nods. He was always happy to leave the divvying up to his brother.

'Then let's be sortin' this Deakin feller out.'

Slouched at the bar, Joe Deakin pushed a dollar bill across the greasy top.

'Whiskey,' he said curtly. 'And make it a double. On second thoughts, I'll take the whole bottle.' Rainbow Tom Pincher, rotund and sporting a shiny bald pate, turned towards the cheaper 'red labels' lined up along the back wall below the long mirror. He had acquired the soubriquet on account of the variety of hues his round face adopted according to his mood. Some customers deliberately riled the bartender just to witness the vibrant performance.

'Not the rotgut,' snapped Deakin. 'Reckon I deserve the best. So let's be havin' the quality stuff.'

'One dollar only buys red label,' huffed the barkeep, evenly holding the other's waspish glower.

Deakin scowled then pushed another greenback across and grabbed the bottle of quality liquor which had been secreted below the counter. His left boot idly toyed with the brass footrail. He splashed a large measure into his glass, downed it in a single gulp and wiped his mouth with the back of a grubby sleeve.

A hot surge launched itself up through his body. Deakin sighed with contentment. This was true 'blue label' bourbon, the real McCoy.

Had he not been hunched over the three-star liquor, perhaps Deakin would have noticed a shadowy figure reflected in the sputtery glow cast by the saloon's only source of illumination, a smoky oil-lamp. Silent as the grave and with a lightness of foot peculiar to bulky men, Caleb Flagg circled behind the distracted youth.

Deakin's attention was totally focused on draining the bottle and working out how he could stretch out the reward money. A twisted grimace splitting the youth's leery visage held little warmth. Maybe he should head for that new silver strike he'd been hearing of down New Mexico way. Maybe join up with some unsuspecting knuckle-head like old Ezra Tindle. But next time he'd make certain of securing the goods before sending the poor sap to meet his maker.

A gravelly voice broke into his dreamy ruminations.

'Yer a thievin' sonofabitch, mister. That reward oughta be shared out.'

Deakin looked up quickly. His drink spilled across the bartop. Quickly recovering his composure, the kid drilled the intruder with a malevolent stare.

'Oh yeh?' he shot back caustically. 'And how d'you figure that?'

'I did my bit. So I reckon you owe me.' Amos Flagg scowled.

'And what does Lassiter and yer big ox of a brother have to say about this?'

'Never mind them,' blustered the miner, drawing himself up. He'd always hated having to look uphill. 'This is between you an' me. Savvy?'

Deakin pushed his wide-brimmed hat to the back of his head surveying the smaller man with a contemptuous smirk.

'And what if I tell you to go stuff yerself?' he growled.

The insult brought a flushed twist to the miner's face. That was when he gave a brief nod. Deakin caught the meaning. But too late.

A huge pair of arms encircled him in a fierce bearhug. He grunted with the sudden tightness as his ribs were squeezed.

'What the hell!' he exclaimed, struggling ineffectually.

Amos Flagg moved in and drove a pair of savage blows to Deakin's stomach. Unable to double up, he gasped in pain. The miner followed through with an equally solid left that shook the young rannie to his foundations. The kid sagged and would have gone down had not Caleb Flagg been pinning him securely. To emphasize they meant business, Amos launched a couple more hard jabs to Deakin's contorted face. Blood poured from a split lip and busted nose.

It was a vicious reminder that just as big fellers could be nimble, small ones compensated with fists of steel.

Caleb let the injured kid fall to his knees. Deakin retched violently.

'Had enough yet?' Amos spat, yanking the kid's head back. A searing backhander sent Deakin crashing against the bar, his breathing harsh and ragged, head spinning. But he was still conscious. And there was no way he was sharing his pay-off. He needed time to think. Time to recover.

'Could be . . . you gotta . . . point,' he gurgled through his smashed mouth. Globules of scarlet dribbled down his chin on to the floor.

Caleb's ugly face split into a toothy grin. His grip slackened.

'Let's be seein' the colour of the *dinero*, kid,' ordered Amos stepping back holding out his hand.

'Help me . . . up,' gasped Deakin, croaking through the pain. His left hand reached for the bartop, the other seeming to reach inside his trousers pocket for the money.

'OK,' replied Amos, 'but no funny business.' He took hold of the bottle of 'blue label' and tipped a hefty slug down his throat.

It was then that Rainbow bent down to retrieve the shotgun he always kept below the counter for just such incidents. Amos Flagg quickly eyeballed the surreptitious manoeuvre.

'Keep yer mits where I can see 'em,' he shouted. His brusque order was backed up by the large Dragoon pointing unerringly at Pincher's bulging midriff. A slight lift of the deadly barrel saw the sweating barkeep reaching for the yellowed ceiling.

That was all the distraction Joe Deakin needed.

He grabbed the neck of the blue label and smashed it down on the counter. The neck crashed off, leaving a ring of wicked fangs blinking in the muted light. With a swift turn he stabbed the lethal jags at Caleb Flagg's brutish face. The big man screamed as a flap of red cheek peeled down. Stumbling away, he fell headlong across a card-table, writhing in agony amidst the debris.

His brother emitted a loathsome howl of fury, swinging the old revolver to bear on his defiant prey. The hammer clicked back ready to spit death. Deakin's eyes popped as he faced a premature get-together with the grim reaper.

SEVEN

PROPOSITION

But the expected roar came from somewhere behind. The gun flew out of Amos Flagg's paw, spinning away to land with a clatter in the gloom. Amos staggered back hugging the numbed appendage.

A decisive command spiked with menace and brooking no retaliation, cut the smoky atmosphere like a knife.

'Now grab that heap of garbage and drift.' The directive, low and even, was uttered by a well-dressed dude.

Unlike the vast majority of Telluride residents, this guy wore a natty blue serge suit with contrasting red silk vest. Muddy brown eyes set a little too close together gave the thin face a shifty mien, an impression supported by the pencil thin moustache. Dandy Jack Brubekker was well named.

What commanded most attention, however, was the smoking Winchester carbine still aimed at the scowling form of Amos Flagg.

'And leave that ancient piece of hardware on the

counter,' added the newcomer firmly.

Flagg reluctantly complied. The carbine then pursued the recalcitrant miner as he assisted his whimpering brother out of the saloon.

'Don't think you've heard the last of this,' Amos called back. The threat sounded rather lame in the circumstances.

Dandy Jack pushed through the batwings, dusted off any loose specks of grit – more for effect than anything else – and smoothed down the crease where the carbine had rested. He sauntered over to the bar.

'Anybody going to offer me a drink?' he said in a marked southern drawl. Deakin was as yet in no position to respond.

'This one's on me, Mr Brubekker,' replied Pincher. Raising a fresh bottle of blue label from below the bar, he nudged it along the counter. 'Them Flagg boys bin askin' fer trouble.' His face lit up like a ripe tomato. 'And you sure gave 'em plenty. Never figured you fer a gunfighter though.'

'Learned my trade in the Fifth Louisiana Light Infantry,' Brubekker offered, sipping at the amber nectar and nodding his appreciation. 'You certainly know a fine bourbon, bartender.'

'Only keep it fer special customers like yerself.'

The sycophantic wheedle was ignored as the dude waited for Deakin to rouse himself. He selected a cheroot from a silver case and bit off the end. The barkeep was quick to respond with a lighted vesta.

It was some ten minutes before the kid dragged himself upright. Dark hooded eyes, one of them half-closed, beheld his benefactor with a glazed frown. Neither man spoke. Why had the guy butted in and saved his hide? He must be after something. Nobody chose to make enemies without a reason. So what was this dude's angle?

Brubekker pushed the bourbon towards the kid.

Deakin accepted the gesture with a curt nod.

'How long you bin standin' by the door, mister?'

'Long enough,' replied Brubekker.

'Then why wait 'til them rats were ready to ship me off to the happy huntin' grounds?' Deakin's tone was questioning rather than challenging. Then he hurried on, 'Not that I'm ungrateful, you understand. But it seems an odd thing to do for someone you never met before. If I were a suspicious feller, I might come to thinkin' you had some underhand reason in mind.'

For a full minute, the natty dude studied the chiselled face, noting the intransigent manner, the icy stare that held his own, the aggressive hostility simmering below the surface. Being a lawyer, Dandy Jack Brubekker possessed the innate ability to read people. And to his mind, this young tearaway exuded the cold arrogance of a born killer.

'I've been watching you, Mr Deakin,' he said, his voice quiet and controlled, compelling even. He drew hard on the cheroot then blew out a tube of thick grey smoke. 'Maybe we can do business.'

Deakin's brow furrowed. Carefully, he assessed the suave dude – the oiled hair flattened to his scalp, black eyes like lumps of coal. Even the polished boots with not a speck of mud visible. This guy oozed success. And Deakin could sure use some of that.

'Maybe,' he replied, assuming an air of casual indifference.

'Then let's you and me wander over to my office.' Brubekker picked up the half-filled bottle of blue label and turned to leave. 'More private over there. Away from nosy bartenders with big ears.' Pincher bridled some but kept his peace. The lawyer had a reputation for 'dealing' with those who ruffled his feathers. 'Well?' The query was aimed at Deakin.

Deliberately holding Brubekker's assured gaze, Deakin straightened his hat and followed the lawyer outside.

Dandy Jack seated himself behind a large desk cluttered with important looking papers fastened with pink ribbons and signalled for Deakin to sit opposite. The kid peered around the room at the shelves chock-full of leather-bound volumes. Brubekker observed the open-eyed surprise etched on the kid's face. Just the kind of naïve impression the lawyer wished to inspire. It gave him the upper hand.

'The law is a complicated business, young feller,' he murmured, lighting up another cheroot. 'It requires a man of letters to understand its intricacies.' Then, in a brisker tone, 'And now to business.'

The lawyer stood up, moved round the desk and sidled over to a large iron safe in the corner.

'The latest model in security devices,' he said proudly, running a hand over the smooth metal surface. 'I had it specially shipped in from Chicago. It would take a wagonload of dynamite to blow this baby open.' Again he patted, almost caressed, the cold hardness of the structure. 'And that's why people come to me with all manner of things they wish to keep out of harm's way. And other people's hands.' A caustic chuckle followed this last remark.

'Come on, mister,' snapped Deakin, his tone brittle and impatient. 'Just git to the point.'

'All in good time, Joe. All in good time.'

Brubekker brushed an imaginary speck of dust from his jacket before continuing: 'As I was saying, folks hand over their most cherished possessions. And in return for the requisite fee, they expect trust and honesty. And I respect that.' He broke off, his brow furrowed, a suggestion of a smile playing across the clean-cut features. 'That is until they pass away without leaving a will.' The smile grew into a full-bodied grin, revealing a set of even white teeth. 'Then I get to thinking. Maybe I should find out just what sort of goods this person was so all-fired eager to keep hidden. Perhaps I could pass them on to a relative. But then again, perhaps not.' He gave a nonchalant shrug of his tapered shoulders.

Deakin gave an exasperated sigh. 'What in thunderation is all this hot air leadin' up to?'

That was when the lawyer played his hand. And what he revealed was a full house.

'Ezra Tindle left a map.'

Deakin tensed. A tremor ran through his taut frame; whether from fear, excitement or a mix of the two, he couldn't figure.

A map!

And that could only mean one thing. The location as to where the nugget was concealed. Deakin smiled to himself. So that was what the old bastard had been up to. Claimed he was going into the mountains on a hunting trip, when all the time. . . .

Deakin rubbed his hands. They felt clammy, tingling with expectation.

Brubekker waited for the momentous revelation to sink

in. Then he made another remark, even more casual than the last, but far more crucial as far as Curly Joe Deakin was concerned.

'It was you that killed Tindle, wasn't it?'

The accusation, uttered in a flat, even tone was concise and damning. Its import struck the kid with the force of a charging buffalo.

'W-w-what kinda play is this,' he stammered weakly. But the protest lacked any fluency. No conviction. 'The killer's in the hoosegow waitin' on the hangman. I-I gave my evidence and the judge commended me for it.'

'No use trying to deny it, kid,' snapped the lawyer, assuming a curt, abrupt manner completely at odds with his previous flippancy. It was a ploy that had worked many times before when dealing with n'er-do-wells in court. 'The old man told me all about you and your idle, shifty ways. Why do you suppose he felt the need to conceal the item in question and leave a map outlining its location in my trustworthy possession. That drifter just happened to be in the wrong place at the wrong time.'

Deakin slumped in his chair, shoulders hunched up in despair. The recently kindled fire had been well and truly doused.

Brubekker pierced him with a baleful smile, straightening his necktie and smoothing back his oiled locks.

'Aren't you going to ask why I brought you here?' he queried pointedly, pacing the small office. 'Not interested to discover why I didn't instantly hand you over to the sheriff? I'd have been doing the community a good turn by preventing a miscarriage of justice.'

Deakin shuffled uneasily, eyeing him, waiting for the lawyer to continue.

'What was that nugget like?' Brubekker asked rather too quickly.

'Ah!' sneered Deakin knowingly, 'that's where this is leadin', is it? You want me to go pick up the trinket and bring it back here. Share out the proceeds.'

'Something like that.'

'So why bring me in on the deal? You could keep it all for yourself,' suggested Deakin, his confidence growing by the second. He reached over and helped himself to a generous slug of the blue label.

'I haven't shown you the map yet,' replied Brubekker. He opened the large safe and removed a buff envelope. Unlike the others stuffed into the heavy strongbox, the red seal had been broken. He removed a grubby sheet of paper and handed it to Deakin.

After perusing the pencilled drawing with its spidery account of the covert location, the kid emitted a deep sigh, jabbing a finger at the map.

'This is mean territory. I passed through Black Canyon last summer heading for Grand Junction. Never met a living soul. Only mountain lions and rattlers live up in that god-forsaken wilderness.'

'That's why I need your help,' interrupted Brubekker. 'You know that country. I don't.'

The kid shot him a suspicious look. 'What's to stop me locatin' the nugget then keep on ridin'.'

A harsh laugh greeted this suggestion. 'Figure me for some kind of greenhorn?'

'What you talkin' about?'

'I'm coming with you.'

Deakin scoffed, squaring his shoulders. 'This ain't gonna be no Sunday-school picnic, mister,' he said. 'Only the tough survive out there. And you don't look so tough to me.'

In the blink of an eye, the lawyer grabbed the kid by the front of his shirt and dragged him upright. The chair went spinning across the room.

'Don't let these fine clothes fool you, kid.' His words hissed out in a rancid growl. 'I eat two-bit gunnies like you for breakfast. So if you're thinking of putting a bullet in my back after we've found the nugget, forget it. I got eyes in the back of my head.'

Deakin flinched as the hooded eyes, black as coal, pierced his brain.

'No offence meant, Mr Brubekker, I just thought you might find it a bit much, that's all.'

'Don't think, kid. Leave all the brainwork to me. That's my business. Savvy?'

Deakin gave an edgy nod.

'Now that we've sorted that out, let's work out the details.' The lawyer assumed his affable persona once again.

It was a little after sun-up the next morning that the unlikely pair of treasure seekers pointed their mounts down Telluride's main drag. A pack-mule trailed behind. Reluctantly, the purpling sky surrendered its hold on the night. Streaks of red paled as the new day broke through.

An early riser might have noticed that Dandy Jack Brubekker had abandoned his dude image in favour of more conventional range garb. The silver-plated Colt Frontier secured round his waist in a fancy tooled holster was somewhat out of keeping with this adopted character. Those unfortunates in the past who had attempted to ridicule the lawyer's choice of protection had met a premature demise and were now pushing up the daisies.

Having cleared the rutted quagmire of the town, they turned east, making towards the Pandoras. Once the soft going across the bottomlands had been negotiated, there followed a laborious climb up past Bridal Veil Falls at the head of the park. In any other state, the glacial trough of the San Juan would have been called a valley, only in Colorado was it a *park*.

Hemmed in by soaring turrets of bare rock, the silvery spout offered an awesome spectacle to be relished by those who didn't have more important things on their minds. Surrounding peaks, still crusted with ice, sparkled in the sunlight, honed to perfection against the cloudless sky.

It was around noon when they emerged from the tree cover into a high-level topography split by meandering gulches. Thrashing watercourses bloated by the spring thaw spluttered and howled across rock-strewn creek beds. Tendrils of rising mist soon dispersed under a strengthening sun.

Progress slowed to a steady plod, allowing the animals to pick their own trail. The tortuous track was becoming rougher as the tree line surrendered to a bleak landscape of crenellated ramparts. Fractured buttresses overhung the trail, threatening to engulf them.

As Brubekker followed in the wake of the kid's snorting mount, he peered around nervously. A town dweller at heart, he had always been uncomfortable faced with the endless wasteland that characterized the Western frontier. His only reason for settling in a cesspit like Telluride was to make money, and lots of it. Once this present caper was concluded, he would make a rapid exit and head for San Francisco.

'How far to this hideaway?' he asked, his voice quiet and subdued.

The kid instantly picked up on the jittery tension.

'Three maybe four days to pack over this range down to Cimarron, then. . . .' He hesitated, sucking in a deep lungful of air.

'Well?'

'We hit Black Canyon,' pronounced Deakin, turning round and aiming a churlish smirk at his new partner. 'That's when we find out how tough you really are . . . *Dandy* Jack.'

EIGHT

DECEPTION

It was getting towards sundown that same day when Paddy McCall drew rein at the entrance to Beaver Dam Pass. Not having encountered another human being since replenishing his supplies three days before at the frontier township of Concord, Paddy was becoming a mite lonesome. He had been on the trail non-stop since leaving the farm the previous week. A kid unused to being alone, this trek into the mountain wilderness of Colorado was stretching his nerves somewhat.

But at the moment he needed fresh meat more than human company. That was his reason for stopping, rabbit offering a tasty change to sowbelly and beans. As he settled down behind a rock, the Hawken primed and ready, his keen eye was suddenly drawn to a twist of grey smoke drifting above a nearby pine grove.

Smoke meant other humans. Whether they were friendly was a different matter. This was where his shiny new Colt would come in handy. Slowly he drew the weapon, flicking the hammer to half-cock, then twirled the cylinder. Satisfied, the kid set his hat straight and took a deep breath.

Edging through the undergrowth, he closed on the other camp with practised silence. Since his pa had lit out, Paddy had become the family hunter. He was proud of the fact that very few nights saw the cooking pot without fresh meat.

It was with a sense of relief that he perceived only one man sitting before the fire. He was poking a stick at a sizzling hunk of bacon. Paddy's nose wrinkled as the aroma struck home. It was a poignant reminder of how hungry he was. Perhaps this dude wouldn't mind sharing his meal. It would save a deal of time waiting on a rabbit to pop its head up. The feller looked harmless enough dressed in a black suit, white shirt and necktie. A shiny black stovepipe hat completed the bizarre attire.

'Hallo the camp!' called Paddy, keeping out of sight just in case. 'Any chance of a cup of that there coffee?'

The man stood up. 'Come along in, stranger,' he called heartily enough. 'Set yourself down. There's bacon on the spit, and beans in the pot.'

Why in tarnation was a dude like this wandering about in such wild and desolate country? The conundrum perplexed Paddy as he unsaddled Spike and set down his bed-roll. The mare immediately moved off in search of succulent greenery by the creek banking.

'Abel Pierpoint.' The introduction was cheery, the handshake firm. It invited a reply.

'Just call me Paddy,' came back the wary response.

'Ah!' breezed the tall man. 'So you hail from the Emerald Isle then?'

'Parents emigrated after the potato famine back in forty-nine,' murmured Paddy, 'I was born an' raised in East Kansas.'

Pierpoint nodded sagely.

Following a few brief pleasantries, the unlikely duo sat down opposite each other to enjoy their makeshift supper. An easy silence settled over the small glade. Paddy idly toed a firebrand, launching a flurry of sparks into the stygian gloom. Surreptitious glances flicked between the unlikely pair across the ethereal shadows cast by the small fire.

But nothing further was said until the unusual traveller passed the makings over to his youthful guest.

That was when curiosity showed its hand at last.

'Headin' far?' asked Paddy casually.

'Telluride,' came back the immediate response. The man drew hard on his thin stogie. Wisps of blue smoke dribbled from the edge of his thin lips.

'How far's that?'

Pierpoint scratched his balding dome. 'Two maybe three days' ride.' He smiled.

'Business?'

'You could say that,' laughed the dude, his skinny frame shaking with obvious mirth. 'Yes indeed, young feller. I certainly have important business that requires my special expertise.'

'What's so funny?' coaxed Paddy, a puzzled frown lining his forehead.

The man's beady eyes sparkled. He refilled his coffee mug and added a generous tot of whiskey, then offered the bottle to Paddy. He nodded towards his saddle resting against the bole of a tree.

'Lariats?' exclaimed the young man, his handsome features screwed into a baffled grimace. 'So?'

'Not just any old ropes,' grinned the dude. 'Those are made from the finest Indian hemp. A professional should have the best tools he can afford. Don't you agree?'

Paddy nodded uncertainly. He was still in the dark – in more ways than one.

Then the truth struck him with the force of a charging bull.

'A hangman!' The realization made him choke on the powerful liquor. An acute fit of coughing threatened him with apoplexy. 'You're a durned hangman?' he finally blurted out.

Pierpoint chuckled loudly. He obviously found the kid's confusion hugely amusing.

'Since we achieved statehood, every hanging has to be conducted official-like.' The gaunt lips spoke with a hint of arrogant pride. 'It's meant a heap of extra business for men in my profession. No more vigilante lynchings.' His nose wrinkled in distaste. 'Them turkeys had no conception of how to do the job properly. It needs finesse, care, and a sympathetic understanding of human nature.'

Pierpoint got to his feet and reached for one of the hanks of new rope.

'Let me show you how a real noose oughta be tied,' he said, fashioning the hemp into the requisite knot and dangling it before his guest's bulging peepers.

Paddy felt a wave of dread surge through his body akin to the cold hand of death.

'My aim is to see a man dispatched within the shortest space of time. The current record is twelve seconds,' stated Pierpoint, nonchalantly caressing his creation.

Paddy could only stare open-mouthed. Never before had he met such a personage. He'd listened to tales about murdering villains being strung up, but life on a remote farm had kept the grisly reality strictly at arm's length.

It took some ten minutes for the young man to recover his composure.

'So who's the unlucky jasper what's gonna git your undivided attention?' he croaked, still ogling the macabre exhibit.

'A guntoter by the name of McCall,' announced the hangman, helping himself to another slug of hooch. Had he witnessed the look of utter amazement breaking over Paddy's face, the guy would have surely been surprised, suspicious even.

But he continued with his exposition, reeling off his account of the felon's crime completely unaware of the hornet's nest he had upset.

'Seems like this Finbar McCall came across a prospector's camp. Blasted the old dude when he refused to surrender his poke.' Pierpoint shook his head, thick eyebrows meeting head on. 'Gruesome business. Judge Took approved the only possible sentence for such a heinous crime.'

Ceremoniously, the man in black laid his right hand on his heart and recited in a stentorian voice the judge's final directive:

'*From here you will be taken to a secure holding, and thence to a place of lawful execution, there to be hanged by the neck until you are dead. And may the Lord have mercy on your soul. Amen.*'

With a flourish he raised the bottle to his lips and drank deep. 'To the soul of Finbar McCall.'

Finbar McCall!

His young brother could barely credit what he was hearing. Colour drained from his normally animated visage. It assumed the appearance of a stony mask, flat and pallid. Thank the stars he had not revealed his own surname.

So Finn was in jail awaiting execution and here was the jigger hired to carry it out.

Always quick on the uptake, Paddy realized he had to take advantage of the situation. His next remark was hardly more than a husky croak.

'Bin to Telluride before, Mr Pierpoint?'

The hangman failed to heed the gutteral rasp.

'First time. My patch is usually to the north around Denver.' His voice was hoarse, the words slurred. He was becoming groggy from too liberal a consumption of his fiery brew. 'And you?'

Paddy ignored the query and heaved a gentle sigh of relief. That meant nobody would know the hangman. His brown eyes glowed in the firelight, determination settling the chiselled features. An owl hooted somewhere in the depths of the forest – a lingering call that floated on the breeze. Scuffles beyond the firelight told him that creatures of the night were abroad. They afforded the tenderfoot sodbuster a poignant reminder of his own vulnerability in this hostile environment.

For some minutes, the two campers stared into the red-and-orange cast by the glowing embers of the fire. Paddy kept arrowing covert glances across the dancing flames, his mind furiously working out a plan of action. The burning twigs crackled and fizzed as his plan began to form. He needed to learn a whole lot more about Abel Pierpoint's terminal profession before the guy passed out.

Especially if he was going to assume the persona of the hangman.

Mud spattered the fetlocks of the large bay as it picked a course down the main street of Telluride. Beneath the black stovepipe, brown eyes keenly surveyed the grim surroundings. Never before had the rider visited a boom-ing gold camp. His nostrils quivered with distaste at the unplanned chaos.

What sort of people would choose to spend their lives in a grim fleapit like this? Miners seeking that elusive gate-way to El Dorado was the obvious answer. For the first time in his life, Paddy McCall yearned for the open flat plains of Kansas. Once regarded as a featureless expanse, his home state was now sown with golden corn crops as far as the eye could see. His dark eyes misted over.

But Paddy was not here to settle down, nor pan for gold. If luck dealt him a winning hand, he and his brother oughta be long gone by this time tomorrow. He could only pray that it would.

Slowing the horse to a walk, he attempted to assimilate everything at a glance. A mange-ridden hound bolted from a side alley, barking frantically at the newcomer. The bay drew to a halt. Gazing up at the black-suited rider, the cur appeared to sense an aura of death accompanying the man and his rope-laden pack-mule. Backing off, it quietly slunk away.

Ever since leaving Beaver Dam Pass two days before, he had been trying desperately to figure out how best to accomplish his task. Not wishing any harm to the hang-man, Paddy had merely ensured the guy was well and truly soused, then removed his clothes. To further hinder the dude's pursuit, he had tossed his boots into the creek. Pierpoint would sure have a mammoth hangover when he eventually awoke. But Paddy knew he would only have a couple of days at the most to free his brother and escape unscathed before the hangman arrived, hell bent on avenging his ignominious shame.

So here he was in Telluride, and still no nearer figuring out a plan of action. Sweat poured down Paddy's face. He wasn't used to thick serge clothing and felt like one of them bandaged Egyptian kings he'd read about. The button-down collar was choking him, the urge to tear it off was overwhelming. Sooner this business was completed the better.

However, Lady Luck had certainly favoured him in one respect. He and Pierpoint were similar in size. Plodding down the street, Paddy was aware of being scrutinized, stared at, even. It wasn't everyday that a hangman came to town. And everyone was looking forward to the grand occasion. Hangings were always an excuse to let off steam.

At the end of the street, a new gallows was at this very moment under construction. Paddy could hear the tap tap tap of hammer on pine. New wood, creamy white and untainted by age, gleamed in the sunlight.

Paddy's jaw dropped. Quickly he realized that an aloof manner would be expected of the official state executioner. He reined in outside the sheriff's office, stepped down from his horse and carefully eyed the growing throng of spectators.

'All set for the big day?' came a jovial call from the rear.

'Can't beat a good neck-stretching.'

A chorus of approval greeted this comment.

'Especially when it's a rat-assed claim-jumper,' added

another voice. The jovial banter instantly changed to a throaty grumble.

Arranging his clothing and setting his hat straight, Paddy cast a supercilious eye over the assemblage. He raised a gloved hand.

'Now, now, gentlemen,' he said loftily. 'No need to get impatient. All in good time. The fellow has to be measured up and weighed first if the job is to be conducted in the correct manner according to the rules laid down by the state legislature. We're all civilized human beings. And even the most villainous criminal deserves a proper send-off, I'm sure you will agree.'

Uttered in the pompous tone he had been practising all day, Paddy was heartily pleased with his performance when the crowd grew silent, hanging on his every word.

'And now, if you please, I have need to consult with the sheriff.' Bowing stiffly and flourishing the stovepipe, he finished with a knowing smile. 'And, of course, my esteemed client.' With a raucous cheer ringing in his ears, the bogus hangman rapped firmly on the office door and stepped inside.

Pinning up a new wanted dodger advertising a reward of $500 for a bank robber with the colourful monicker of Flatnose Jim Ekker, the sheriff was momentarily taken by surprise. He gaped at the black apparition. Quickly recovering, he warily moved to greet the newcomer, a cautious hand resting on the butt of his pistol.

'Abel Pierpoint, sir,' announced Paddy firmly, extending his hand, 'state hangman here to officiate at the coming event.'

The sheriff relaxed but shot the newcomer an intense look.

'Bit young, ain't you?' he muttered in a disparaging tone.

Paddy drew himself up to his full height of six feet two and aimed a caustic eye at the smaller man.

'If you are concerned as to my competence in this delicate matter, I have here letters of reference testifying to my ability to dispatch the subject humanely and with complete satisfaction to all concerned.' He reached into his inside pocket and removed an official-looking envelope. A candid stare held the lawman, challenging him to make an issue of the matter. 'The state governor has received no complaints thus far.'

'No offence meant, Mr Pierpoint.' stuttered the lawman, anxious to cover his discomfiture. 'Welcome to Telluride.' He accepted the proferred hand. 'Can I offer you a cup of coffee?'

'Later if you don't mind, Sheriff,' said Paddy in a looser vein. The last thing he wanted was to enter into a protracted discussion on legal matters with the local tin star. 'I have come a long way today and would prefer to meet with my client first.' He sidled towards the cellblock door.

'Hold on there, mister,' called out Montane in a slightly condescending tone which brought the other man to an abrupt halt. 'If you're so all-fired good, then you oughta know the rules.'

Paddy stiffened. What did the guy mean? What rules?

'Just testing you, Sheriff.' The breezy smile cracking Paddy's face was anything but natural. He forced himself to remain calm. 'Just testing. Can't be too careful with a dangerous felon locked up now, can we?'

Thankfully, Montane accepted the check. He took the initiative.

'Arms in the air if you will, Mr Pierpoint.'

Paddy complied. Then the sheriff frisked him for any concealed weapons. He removed the Peacemaker from its holster.

'You're certainly right there,' he agreed, nodding his head vigorously. 'Cain't be too careful. You're free to visit with your client now.'

'Much obliged, sir.'

Paddy turned away to hide the relief that would surely have given him away. Montane stepped in front, leading the way into the narrow corridor behind. There were two cells, each with a heavy steel barred door. Only one of them was occupied. The resident was lying on a grubby cot, hands behind his head puffing on a roll-up.

He angled a surly gaze at the lawman.

'A visitor for you.' Montane grinned disdainfully.

The prisoner remained silent.

'This feller needs to take down your measurements.' Montane slung a thumb to his rear. 'And not for a new suit neither. Where you're headed, a wooden overcoat'll do.' He uttered a hoarse chuckle at his jocularity before addressing the man in black. 'You got ten minutes, mister.'

'Thank you, Sheriff,' Paddy said, concealing a grim scowl. 'That will be sufficient for my purpose.'

He waited until the lawdog had returned to the front office, then addressed the prisoner in the official tone of his adopted profession, thumbs hooked into his vest pockets.

'Kindly be upstanding, my good fellow, so that I can dispense with the formalities as quickly as possible.'

Finn lay on the cot ignoring the request and pulling the wide-brimmed hat further over his eyes.

Paddy gave a sharp cough.

Still no reaction.

Only then did Paddy continue in his normal cadences, though in a subdued whisper so as not to alert the sheriff.

'Ain't you gonna say howdie then . . . brother?'

Finn tilted the hat back, his dark eyes peered from beneath the brim, widening perceptibly as he recognized his younger brother. His mouth gaped wide. For a brief instant he stared at the apparition, utterly dumbfounded. Then he was on his feet, both hands grasping the bars so tightly the knuckles blanched.

'Where did you spring from?' he gasped out at last. 'And what's all this?' He pointed at the black suit and tall hat.

'Not so loud! That lawdog is one suspicious dude.'

'How d'you find me?' From abject despair, Finn's mood was now one of elation. He pressed his brother for answers.

'When you never sent word, Ma an' me got to thinkin' the worst,' Paddy said hurriedly. Then in a few concise sentences he outlined his trek west and how he had met up with the official hangman, and had then assumed his identity. He finished with the warning that: 'Once the guy gets his head together, he'll ride like the devil to put things to rights. So we definitely need to be eatin' dust by this time tomorrow.'

Time, as they say, was of the essence. And once the first euphoria had passed, both men simmered down, acknowledging the gravity of their situation. The clock was ticking and there was much to be done.

Whilst filling his brother in on developments, Paddy had been desperately trying to formulate a plan of action.

There had to be a way out. He had the whip hand which must count for something. Tense eagle eyes swept round the confined space of the cell block. Bare walls of dried red mud were scrawled with messages left by previous inmates. An empty tin plate and mug lay on the dirt floor.

And it smelled foul, most of the rank odour emanating from a slop bucket in the corner.

'That thing ever emptied?' Paddy's nose curled.

'Once a day is all.'

Paddy was about to comment further when an idea suddenly presented itself, a bolt from the wide blue yonder: the abrupt realization that hard, sun-baked mud could easily be dug away with a sharp blade. Bending down, Paddy quickly extracted a sheathed Bowie knife from inside his right boot. He passed it through the bars to his brother. Finn immediately slid the deadly blade beneath his pillow.

Paddy threw a quick glance at the closed office door.

'Soon as I've gone, you git to work on them window bars.' His voiced exuded a nervous inflection matching the wary eyes that glinted with suppressed anxiety. 'Just before daybreak,' he continued hurriedly, 'I'll come round to the back and fasten the hangin' ropes round 'em. Then with God's help and a pair of strong cayuses, we should be outa here pronto.' He peered at the silver pocket-watch in his vest. 'Two in the afternoon. That oughta give you plenty of time to git them bars nice and shaky. I'll head down to the livery stable and rent a twin-rigged buckboard. That oughta fit the job,' continued Paddy with an exaggerated confidence, adding pointedly: 'You just make sure them damn bars is well loosened.'

'You packin' any hardware?' said Finn.

'The old Hawken and a new short-barrel Peacemaker I bin practisin' with.' Paddy's face lit up with pride. 'I can hit four out of five tin cans at twenty paces from the draw.'

'What about when it comes to the real thing,' observed Finn in a hard edged rasp. 'You got the bottle, junior?' As head of the household once his father had left home, Finn had taken it upon himself to be the paternal guardian of his younger brother. Sometimes it irked, especially now that the kid was having to bust him out of jail.

'Didn't I come all this way,' he blazed, cheeks flushed and eyes burning red at the slight, 'and for what? To dig you outa the pokey. So don't come on all high and mighty with me, *brother*.'

'OK, simmer down,' urged Finn, concerned that a raised voice would alert the sheriff. 'Think I don't appreciate it? 'Course I do.'

Paddy shot a quick glance behind on hearing a chair scrape in the outer office. Both men stiffened. Soon after, Montane tugged open the heavy cell-block door.

'Finished in here then?' he enquired.

'I have indeed, Sheriff,' trilled Paddy in his official voice, casually stepping back from the barred cell door. 'We'll have this fellow stoking up the fiery furnace with Old Nick himself this time tomorrow.' Paddy's next remark was aimed at the prisoner. 'Much obliged for your co-operation, Mr McCall. It will be my pleasure to ensure you receive a swift and neat departure.' A crafty wink passed between the two brothers. 'And I am certain you will be well satisfied with the outcome.'

'Go to hell,' snarled Finn, slamming a bunched fist against the bars.

'Not doubt I will, sir,' came back the flippant response.

'No doubt at all.' Then Paddy returned to the front office, addressing the sheriff in a breezy lilt. 'And now for that cup of finest Arbuckle you promised me. Perhaps with a small nip?' Montane obliged from a bottle he kept in his desk. 'Just to keep out the cold you understand . . . and only the one, mind. I need to check out the gallows and trapdoor. Must keep a clear head. But at least the prisoner is a heavy-set fellow so he won't be needing extra weight.'

Montane shot him a quizzical glance.

'Small light men need a helping hand, sir,' offered the 'hangman' for explanation, 'else they kick and struggle for ages.' He shook his head emphatically. 'Most distressing. And most unprofessional, I'm sure you will agree.'

'Yeh, sure,' mumbled the sheriff. 'Just so long as the jasper gets his neck stretched I ain't a-carin' how it's done.'

'Not quite the attitude we like to see in our law officers,' chided Paddy.

Montane snorted with indignation. Who did this jumped-up squirt think he was. He opened his mouth to spit out a caustic retort. Just in time, the lawman forced himself to curb his resentment. These dudes had clout with the state authorities and Jake Montane liked this job. Any case, the guy would be out of his hair in a couple of days.

Wrapped up in his world of make-believe, Paddy failed to notice the sheriff's sullen demeanour. He was really beginning to enjoy himself. Perhaps he should apply for the job when this business was over. Then he caught sight of the dark scowl, the rigid stance. And suddenly, Paddy McCall remembered where he was and what still had to be done. The thought jerked him back to reality.

Busting someone out of jail would put him on the owl-hoot trail. Well and truly on the run from the law. But what choice did he have? None. His brother was innocent and due to hang the following day. Fresh air and a square meal were needed to help bring some degree of order to the chaotic feelings rustling about inside his head.

'Can you suggest a suitable eating establishment?' he asked, making for the front door.

'Try the Pancake House across the street,' replied Montane sourly. 'Josie Green is the best cook in town. She might even give you a room for the night.'

'Obliged, Sheriff.'

But Montane had already turned away, fiddling with some papers on his scarred desk: his way of dismissing the hangman. Already he was thinking about Curly Joe Deakin. He hadn't seen him for a few days. Maybe he'd just lit out for pastures new now his partner was dead.

Montane shrugged. Good riddance.

NINE

BREAKOUT!

Paddy was sitting at a table by the window studying the menu card when a rich Southern nuance struck him in the right ear.

'What'll it be then, mister?'

Clutching a small pad and pencil and waiting to take his order was a tall raven-haired woman in her middle thirties. Her gingham dress matched the neat curtains. But it was the more than ample bosom straining beneath the white blouse that drew his eye.

This must be Josie Green. Lusty male patrons ogling her assets was no new experience for the Texan belle.

'And its food only that's on the menu,' she snapped, holding his stare. Paddy's face reddened and he turned away quickly, burying his face in the menu.

'W-what's the house special?' he stuttered.

'Beef stew and dumplings,' came back the firm response.

'I'll have that with a pot of coffee.' He offered her rear

a nervous glance as the woman disappeared into the kitchen. Only then did he relax.

After the meal, while he was enjoying a smoke with his coffee, the proprietor came over to clear away his plate. Paddy coughed to break the tension. This female made him nervous, and not just because she'd rebuked him.

'A fine dinner, madam,' he said.

'New in town?' she enquired, ignoring the compliment.

Paddy nodded, falling naturally into his role. 'Abel Pierpoint, the state hangman, at your service. Here in Telluride to officiate at the event on the morrow.'

Hands on hips, Josie regarded him charily. 'I figured you for a much older man, Mr Pierpoint. My uncle runs the law enforcement agency for south-west Colorado. Seems like you and he are *old* friends.' Here she paused, a dark expression clouding her smooth features. 'I received a letter only last week to say he would be arriving on tonight's stage from Durango.'

Tight-jawed, Paddy struggled to remain impassive. He hesitated fractionally before replying, 'And what time is the stage due in?'

'Around ten o'clock,' she said, running a sceptical gaze over the man in black.

'It will be good to meet up again after all this time,' he bluffed pushing his chair back to rise. 'But first I have certain preparations that need my attention.'

'Another coffee before you hurry off, Mr Pierpoint?' The sardonic inflection was not lost on the young impostor, her green eyes gently mocking.

'I would love to stop and talk, Miss Green.' He smiled, throwing a handful of dollar bills on to the table. 'But time stops for no man as they say.' He hurriedly left the premises with the pompous effrontery to invite her to 'keep the change.'

Outside, the late afternoon sun was beating a hasty retreat from a cloudless sky. But all Paddy McCall felt was a cold hand squeezing at his innards. That blasted woman, she must have figured something wasn't right. No open accusation, just a niggling suspicion.

Why couldn't a younger man be friendly with her uncle? But the question remained: what would she do now? The most likely option would be to wait for her uncle to arrive. Ask him to describe Pierpoint. Then all hell would break loose.

He stumbled off down the street, anxious for some breathing space. An opportunity to collect his thoughts. This revelation changed everything. The break-out would have to take place before the stage arrived if they were to have any chance of getting clear. He peered at the watch – it read 4.17 p.m.

Less than six hours.

The blanched expression, pinched and haggard for one so young, attracted a few curious stares. Even concerned comments.

'You OK, mister?' from one old guy. Paddy offered a brief shake of the head then hurried on. The last thing he wanted now was the whole town muttering implications about the *young* hangman, and his not having the bottle for such a terminal occupation.

Opposite the jailhouse, a wave of nausea surged up through his guts. Forcing himself to stay calm and think straight, Paddy slunk down a side-alley beside two stores. Away from prying eyes.

He needed to get a grip on himself. And fast.

The first thing was to warn Finn. Slanting a wary eye up and down the length of the main street, he waited until the coast was clear, then hustled across to the sheriff's office. He hesitated outside to gather himself, then knocked purposefully on the door.

'Come in, then,' echoed a surly gripe from inside.

A cup raised to his mouth, Montane was having a late meal.

'Figured I'd seen the last of you for today,' he muttered chewing on a hunk of bread. Stray bits of meat clung precariously to his grey whiskers.

'I need to see the prisoner again.'

'What fer?' grumbled Montane, wiping the gravy from his chin. 'No hangin' I ever attended before was this complicated.'

Nevertheless, he hauled his ass out of the chair.

'New regulations, Sheriff,' responded Paddy vigorously, struggling to contain his impatience. 'State legislature wants everything done right now we're part of the Union.'

'Umph!' The sheriff was clearly a man of the old school.

'I only need five minutes,' wheedled Paddy, sidling towards the rear of the office. The sheriff moved in front, not so old as to forget the customary search. Then he unlocked the door.

'Five minutes and no longer,' he rasped, heading back to his abandoned meal. 'I want to shut this place up tighter 'n a banker's fist. Nobody comes in or out 'til you're ready fer doin' yer duty tomorrow.' With that prophetic reminder, the door slammed shut.

Now the two brothers were alone.

'Bad news,' rapped Paddy in a harsh undertone.

'What?'

'There's some legal feller arrivin' on the night stage,' Paddy gulped, breath rasping in his throat.

'Calm down and tell it straight,' urged Finn, gripping his brother's arm. 'No sense gettin' into a lather. So who is this dude?'

'That's the point,' cut in Paddy. 'The owner of the cook-house over the road reckons him an' me are old buddies. That's why we have to be well outa here before ten. That's when the stage is due in.'

Finn's brow creased in alarm. Outside a dog howled as if in sympathetic accord.

'How you doin' with them bars?' asked Paddy, casting a worried look at the rear window.

'Slow job.' Finn sighed. His shoulders sagged. Was this to be the end of the line?

Paddy sensed his brother's anguish. His own brow knit-ted in thought.

'We still have five hours,' he said, trying to imbue a measure of confidence into his words. 'With this place locked up, you won't have to worry about makin' a racket. And after sundown, I'll come round the back and help from the outside.' He gripped Finn's arm firmly. 'No way am I gonna let them hang you. We're partners ain't we?'

Eyes glazing over, Finn nodded sombrely. Not from fear, but gratitude that his kid brother was willing to risk all. They were indeed partners now. But Finn was well aware that if they did escape, it would mean a life on the run for them both. Dodging the law for the rest of their lives.

Unless he could prove his innocence.

Imbued with a fresh spirit of resolve, Paddy strode off along the boardwalk. His destination was the livery stable at the edge of town to hire the buckboard. Heavy droplets of rain tapping on the stovepipe soon developed into a steady downpour. Paddy turned up his collar and hurried on. A smile split his dour features. Rain drove people inside. It would make his job that much easier.

'Plan on stickin' around after the hangin'?' enquired the ostler, leading out a pair of chestnut mares from their stalls.

'It's my intention to have a house built up the trail apiece,' replied Paddy positively. 'I need this wagon to move supplies.'

The old man grunted but said no more as he prepared the rig.

'Keep these ladies on a short rein,' he advised as Paddy climbed up and took his seat. 'Like all females, they get a mite fidgety if allowed too much freedom.' He handed the loose reins over, adding, 'Want to borrow my slicker? Save you from a soakin'.'

'Much obliged,' replied Paddy, accepting the offer. No sense taking a dousing if it could be avoided. He slipped the yellow coat over his suit, gave the man a final wave, then drove out of the corral, turning south away from the grim reality of Telluride.

'Woodyard's at the other end of town,' shouted the ostler, gesticulating with both arms. But the cry was whisked away by the noise of splashing hoofs churning up the trail mud. The old guy shrugged and returned to his duties.

Paddy figured the less time he spent in town while it was still light, the better. After a couple of miles, he pulled the buckboard off the trail under a rocky overhang offering a measure of protection from the incessant deluge. Pulling out a silver hip flask from a pocket, the lad peered at the inscription. *To Abel with fondest love – Rachel.* He unscrewed the cap and took a deep draught of finest three star French brandy. Unused to hard liquor, his stomach threatened to evict the intrusive fire. But following another slug, the raging inferno mellowed to a warm glow that suffused his whole body. It was sure better than any camp fire to keep the chill at bay.

The next two hours passed in a haze of alcoholic delirium. Only when he attempted to alight from the buckboard to relieve himself did the realization of how much he'd drunk hit Paddy with stunning force. Tumbling in the dirt jarred him out of the stupor. More by luck than good judgement he managed to avoid the stomping hoofs of the frightened team. The shock brought him rapidly to his senses. He staggered over to a small creek at the trailside plunged his inebriated head into the freezing water.

The effect was immediate. Still under the influence, at least he was able to think in a coherent manner, even if his movements were a mite jerky.

He scanned the timepiece. Time to move.

To avoid the main thoroughfare of Telluride, Paddy deliberately returned to town via a back trail. Approaching from the north, it was hemmed in by dense thickets of dwarf oak and willow. Too small for use in the mines, they had been left alone and now afforded a welcome screen. Soon, the buckboard was into a disorganized array of tin huts and canvas lean-tos where the less successful residents of the town lived. Abandoned tailings littered the uneven terrain around which the rough trail meandered. Every now and then small creatures with long tails skipped across in front of the wagon.

Rats! Paddy shivered. He hated rats.

Hauling back the skittish pair of chestnuts to a walk, he nervously flicked a cautious eye over the rear of the more permanent structures backing on to main street. Nothing moved. A rare silence appeared to engulf the town. It was a period of limbo before the hectic distractions of the night hours began.

Slowly he approached the back wall of the hoosegow. Easy to pick out even in the dusky gloom of early evening, the flat red of smoothed adobe contrasted with the drab weariness characteristic of unpainted wood.

Another quick glance round and Paddy was at the barred window. Thankfully the rain had stopped just as the full moon slid effortlessly behind a cloud bank.

'Finn!' he hissed urgently, 'You there?' A pointless enquiry. His brother had no other invitations in his diary. Except with the real hangman if this venture failed.

'Here, junior,' came back the hoarse whispered reply. 'I bin hard at work with this here Bowie. But it's a slow process.'

'I'll draw the buckboard up to the window. It'll be easier diggin' out the clay from this side.' Paddy stepped on to the tailboard and peered through the inch-thick iron bars, giving his brother a reassuring smile. On the outside of the jail, the crumbly red adobe had peeled off under the incessant hammering of the sun to reveal the rough texture of brickwork beneath. Using a pitchfork he'd found, Paddy jabbed the sharp prongs into the gaps, levering out chunks of mortar.

'Soon have you outa here, brother,' he said. Then paused to listen intently.

A couple of blocks down from the jail, in a room out back of the Silver Dollar, Jackdaw Lassiter was stirring. He grunted, then belched loudly, shrugging off the after-effects of his liquid supper. Scratching at his swollen belly, the saloon bum lumbered to his feet not forgetting the half-empty bottle of red label. He jammed an ageing derby on his head and opened the back door. Then he trundled off through the maze of stinking alleys that spread out like a festering sore behind Telluride's main drag.

Still half-cut, Lassiter whistled a tuneless ditty as he splashed unheeding through the numerous mud pats. To reach the squalid hovel that he called home, the drunk had to pass the rear of the jailhouse. He had decided to have a bit of fun at the expense of the prisoner.

The moon chose that particular moment to peek out from the clouds, bathing the landscape in a shadowy radiance. What he saw stopped him in his tracks. Even Jackdaw Lassiter's addled brain couldn't fail to comprehend the bizarre tableau.

Could that really be the state hangman picking at the wall with a pitchfork? Lassiter shook his head to clear the demons. His rheumy eyes had not deceived him.

'What the hell is goin' on here?' he called, scrabbling for an old cap and ball Army Remington stuck in his belt. So engrossed was Paddy in his task that he dropped the fork. Luckily, the long barrel of Lassiter's pistol had snagged on his buckle. With the drunk struggling to dislodge his gun, Paddy immediately launched himself at the approaching threat. Both men crashed to the ground, rolling about in the dirt.

Over and over they tumbled, each striving for the ascendancy. That meant coming out on top. Even Jackdaw Lassiter, his brain still dulled by rotgut whiskey, recognized this for a fact. He was a burly hulk of a man, more flab than muscle, but Paddy stood no chance of heaving the leaden weight off his slim torso.

Lassiter smirked, a mean glint in his bloodshot eyes.

'This is where you git yours, mister.' He drew back his right arm and aimed a piledriver at the youngster's creased face.

'I allus figured there was somethin' not right about you,' he growled. 'Too damn young for a neck-stretcher.'

Just in time, Paddy wrenched his head sideways. The stunning blow flew past, grazing his temple. Had it landed, the contest would have been over. Instead, Lassiter's fist connected with a loose rock. Yelling in pain, he lifted his ponderous bulk slightly, rubbing at the injured appendage.

That was all Paddy needed. Mustering his strength, he rammed his left knee upwards into the drunk's exposed groin. Lassiter grunted, a harsh rasp escaping from pursed lips. It was a jolting blow, but insufficient to deflate the hulk. A second lunge struck Lassiter with full-ball force. This time, the drunk emitted an agonized groan and slumped sideways cradling his mangled vitals.

In an instant Paddy was on his feet. Backing off he grabbed for his own holstered revolver.

Finn had been avidly watching the action from the cell window, his knuckles a deathly white as they gripped the bars. The shadowy tussle seemed like a ghostly nightmare in the pale moonlight. He glanced up at the surrounding

89

back windows. There were a few yellowish glimmers but nobody so far appeared to have heard anything that warranted investigation.

'Don't shoot him!' Finn's hoarse undertone made the lad hesitate. 'You'll have the whole town buzzin' round our ears.'

Though somewhat the worse for wear, Lassiter was not about to give up now. He had visions of a grateful town plying him with the finest blue label well into the summer. A rabid growl issued from a dry throat as he prepared for one mighty lunge.

'Use the pitchfork!' hissed Finn.

Breathing hard, his brother desperately tried to penetrate the stygian gloom, one hand still clutching the butt of his Peacemaker. Where was the damn blasted thing?

'On the ground by the back wheel!'

Finn's fretful bark saw Paddy floundering near the tailgate of the buckboard just as the big man lunged towards him. Lassiter's own pistol was out, the barrel rising. The click of the drawn hammer echoed loudly in the confines of the alley. Bending down on one knee, Paddy gripped the wooden shaft and swung the twin-pronged fork towards the threatening hulk.

At that moment, the grim reaper beckoned invitingly. The young farmer ignored the invitation.

A coarse snarl came from deep in his throat as the drunken man saw the wicked steel barbs thrusting urgently at the approaching death threat. Too late, Jackdaw Lassiter himself witnessed the welcoming smile of the scythe man. The momentum of his stumbling lunge booked him a permanent site on Boot Hill. Grey eyes bulged as the lethal spikes bit deep, penetrating the fleshy torso to their full length. His mouth fell open, a crimson trickle staining the dirty beard.

One final thrust and Lassiter staggered back, twitching muscles grabbing at the pitchfork. He slammed back against the side of a building and slid to the ground, glazed eyes still wide and staring.

Dragging in ragged gasps of air, Paddy clutched at his stomach. Then he emptied his dinner into the nearest puddle. Grovelling in the mud on hands and knees, his innards retched painfully. This was the first time he'd killed a human being. And it was not the simple task depicted in the numerous dime novels he had so avidly devoured back home. At that precise moment, the dull routine and hard graft of scraping out a meagre living on a dirt farm seemed like a utopian paradise.

But this was no time for rueful reflection.

'It was him or you.' Finn was quick to remind him. 'But we ain't got time fer speculatin' on the matter. Someone might happen along at any minute. Fasten them ropes to the bars and the buckboard tailgate.'

Paddy remained still, unmoving. His heart pounded against his ribcage, threatening to bust out. Finn recognized that his brother was in shock. Drastic action was needed if their plan was to have any chance of success.

His head disappeared from the barred window. A moment later he reappeared clutching a tin mug. He threw it at his brother, the metal clanged on the iron rim of the rear wheel, then struck Paddy on the back of the head.

But the noise coupled with the lethal fracas was more than sufficient to arouse interest elsewhere. A back upstairs window creaked open and a tousled head appeared.

'What in tarnation's all the racket down there?' grumbled an irate voice. 'Can't a guy enjoy a bit of peace an' quiet in this hell-hole fer once.'

That was enough to jerk Paddy out of the dazed torpor. Luckily for him, the moon chose that moment to slip back behind a wandering cloud, once again throwing the alley into pitch darkness. In total silence, he crawled behind the buckboard and waited. Figuring the noise must have been made by bickering cats, the man grunted and closed the window.

Briefly scanning both ends of the alley for any sign of further interruptions, Paddy gave his brother the thumbs-up and proceeded to secure the two ropes. When he'd finished, there was about twelve feet of slack.

'Listen up now, brother,' said Finn as the last knot was tied. 'Once them horses start to heavin' on their reins, there's gonna be more racket than any old tin cup. So we gotta move fast.'

'So this is it,' muttered Paddy, his voice crackling with suppressed tension.

Finn merely nodded, offering his brother a spirited look of reassurance. They clasped hands through the bars. Then Paddy stepped away from the back wall of the jail and settled himself on the front seat of the buckboard.

TEN

WESTWARD

Grasping the reins and leather switch, Paddy slapped the rump of the lead horse and let out a raucous yip. Instantly the pair of frisky cayuses bounded forward, straining their haunches when the ropes tightened. Rearing up on hind legs, they whinnied and snorted through foam-flecked nostrils.

'Yahooooh!' urged Paddy flailing the reins. Finn joined in. It was now all or nothing.

Suddenly, a cracking and grinding of adobe clay drowned out the strident cacophony. The back wall was disintegrating.

'Stand back!' yelled Paddy, urging the horses to greater efforts. 'It's about to give way.'

As if released from a bow, the horses and buckboard shot forwards, dragging out a section of red walling about three feet square. Dust and fragments of clay blew out from the jagged gash in the cell wall, or what was left of it. Paddy immediately hauled back on the reins and jammed his foot on the brake. He jumped down and quickly untied the ropes.

Coughing and spluttering, his bandanna held up to his face, Finn McCall emerged through the shifting wreckage. Even in the heat of the moment, with escape of paramount importance, he remained sufficiently calm to urge his brother to help lift the deceased drunkard on to the buckboard. No sense advertising to the town that one of their own had met a grisly end.

Even in a rip-roaring berg like Telluride, where rowdy antics were the norm, the unholy clamour they had raised was bound to attract attention. Morbid curiosity had attracted a horde of spectators for the hanging. The saloons would soon be crowded. Everyone would be getting themselves liquored up for the grand hoohah.

Finn scrambled up on to the front of the buckboard, joined two ticks later by his brother. He glanced quickly back to the entrance of the alley. Already a yelling mob was gathering. Unsure as to the source of the sudden pandemonium, they still had not associated it with the jailhouse. Above the bellicose yammering, Finn made out the gruff bark of Sheriff Montane urging those nearest to check the rear and report back to him.

'Time to make ourselves scarce,' hollered Finn, no longer bothering to keep silent. 'Whip them cayuses good an' let's split the breeze.'

'Which way?' replied Paddy.

'Through tent city and the old tailings,' Finn shot back, keeping a nervous eye on his rear. The hard edge to his voice urged Paddy onward. 'We can swing back towards the main trail further west. That oughta fox 'em fer a spell. It'll give us enough time to hunker down some place.' He coughed thickly then hawked a gut-full of red phlegm into the darkness.

'You OK?' asked Paddy.

'Never better, junior.' A broad grin wide as the Old Missouri split Finn's handsome visage. 'Never better.'

Boy, it felt good to be free again. But for how long? He knew they would have to ditch the buckboard and find some proper saddle-horses if they were to make good their escape with a posse breathing down their necks.

Paddy appeared to read his thoughts.

'Look behind,' he said with a wry smirk creasing his mouth.

'Eh?'

'In the well next to that heap o' shit,' pressed Paddy, poking a thumb behind him.

Finn looked round. His eyes bulged in amazement. Two saddles complete with full tack lay side by side.

'Figured we might be needin' 'em,' snickered Paddy with an affected air of careless nonchalance.

'You goldarned son-of-a-gun!' Finn threw out a hearty laugh, slapping his brother playfully on the back.

'I recognized your mount from the Triple K brand it was carryin',' continued Paddy. 'Somebody must have taken it to the livery stable after you'd bin jailed. While the ostler was sortin' out the bridles and harness, I lifted your saddle pack and stowed it under a tarp.'

Finn chuckled gleefully. 'What would I do without you?'

Then with a single voice, as if on cue, they both broke into a rumbustious bout of cheering. Boots stamping wildly, they clung precariously to its springy bench seat as the rig careered on its way, twisting and weaving through the chaotic conglomeration of shanties. In a matter of

minutes, the town had been left behind. Only then did
Paddy give the horses their heads. An occasional flick of
the switch kept them at the gallop when they attempted to
slacken pace. At that moment, speed was more important
than anything else.

Ghostly clusters of thorn and sagebrush flashed by. The
occasional barking of a coyote added to the frenetic
scenario. Thankfully the moon had seen fit to make
another reappearance, bathing the trail in its ethereal
glow.

A little under an hour later, Finn picked out the outline
of a bucking vehicle coming towards them. He dug an
elbow into his brother's ribs.

Paddy stiffened.

'It must be the night stage from Durango,' he observed,
tight-lipped.

Finn drew the rig to the side of the trail, allowing the
coach to pass. A casual wave was reciprocated by the unsuspecting driver. Inside he noted a distinguished older man
with a grey beard and sporting a single eyepiece. This
must be Josie Green's uncle. The man barely gave them a
glance. If only he knew the truth. That state of affairs
would be rectified soon enough.

Another two hours of hard riding, with only brief
stops to ease the horses, and Finn called a halt, instruct-
ing his brother to pull off the trail into a clump of
willow. The steaming mounts bucked and snorted, grateful for the rest. When Paddy made to question him, Finn
held up a stiff hand. He removed his hat, stepped down
from the buckboard and cocked an ear to their back
trail. For a full minute he listened hard, sifting the
multitude of sounds that permeated the darkness, trying

to determine whether a posse was on their tail.

Eventually he relaxed, leaned back against the side of the buckboard and rolled a smoke. Paddy joined him, rubbing his ass vigorously to ease the stiffness.

'Think we've shaken 'em?' inquired Paddy anxiously.

'For the time bein'.' Finn drew the smoke deep into his lungs. A rueful expression beetled his puckered brow. 'I figure we should be all right 'til sun-up. That sheriff won't have cottoned on to which direction we took with the main trails so well rutted. But at first light, he'll be on our case with a vengeance. That's when riders will be sent out to scout around. Now that we've pulled off the main drag, these wheel rims will leave a trail a blind man could follow.'

'We'll have to dump the wagon, then,' surmised Paddy.

'Not forgettin' it's gruesome cargo,' added Finn wrinkling his nose.

'You figure we oughta make camp around here?'

Finn nodded thoughtfully. 'At first light we'll brush out the wheel marks where the rig pulled off the trail.'

'It'll have to be a dry camp then.'

'You got it, kid. Can't afford to give away our position with a fire. You guide the 'board up this draw. We can cover it with brushwood before we leave.'

'That oughta give us some breathing space at least,' agreed Paddy. Gently he coaxed the team between tangled banks of willow and thorn scrub.

A half-mile off the main trail, he drew to a halt. He released the horses from their leathers and saddled them both ready for an early start the next morning. Before they could settle down for the night there was one last job still to be completed. And not the pleasantest of tasks, either.

Working together, it took their combined efforts to lift the bulky corpse of Jackdaw Lassiter off the buckboard and sling it over one of the horses. The moon had reached its highest point, creating sufficient light for the brothers to pursue the task of secreting their gruesome burden.

They found the ideal spot a hundred yards further along the draw. A narrow ravine where the rock had been split as if by a blow from some giant axe blade fell away abruptly on their left. Barely more than the width of a man's shoulders, it was impossible to see the bottom in the eerie gloom.With Paddy grasping the big man by the shoulders and Finn taking the legs, they manhandled the dead weight over to the yawning chasm and pushed it over the edge. Panting from the exertion, they listened carefully. Finn counted off five seconds before a dull thud informed him that Lassiter had hit the bottom of the ravine.

'Reckon it'll be judgement-day before he's discovered,' announced Finn, breathing heavily.

'If'n the prairie dogs don't git to him first.'

For Paddy McCall, the night passed in a series of fitful dreams. It wasn't everyday you killed a man then dumped his body unceremoniously into some black hole in the ground. He was relieved when the murky shadows of the false dawn eventually heralded the start of a new day.

'Sleep well?' asked Finn brightly. He had no such conscience about saving himself from the hangman's unwelcome ministrations.

Paddy grunted negatively, then rolled out of his blanket.

'You shouldn't lose any sleep over spikin' that saloon bum,' Finn chided, passing his brother a chunk of dried jerky beef.

'It weren't you what done the killin',' rasped Paddy testily, chewing on the tough meat. It tasted like boot leather. He took a swig of water from his canteen. At that moment he would have given anything for a cup of hot Arbuckles.

'Time we was on the move.'

Finn checked the saddle trappings of the chestnut mare, adjusting straps as needed. Meanwhile, the horse chewed on a clump of gramma grass ignoring the attention. He removed the trusted Henry repeating carbine from the saddle boot, then checked the load, levering fresh cartridges into the slide breech. A quick spin of the Navy's cylinder assured him the revolver was primed, then he slipped it back into the holster.

'Best check your hardware too,' Finn advised his brother. He mounted up and nudged the animals back towards open terrain. Ground hitching the chestnut behind a craggy promontory, he climbed to the top and surveyed the broken country back east in the direction of Telluride.

Nothing stirred in the early morning haze. He let out a sigh of relief.

Below the vantage point, Paddy had hacked off a hazel branch and was sweeping loose sand into the deep ruts cut by the wagon.

'Appears like we've given 'em the slip,' announced Finn with a broad smile.

'For now maybe,' mumbled Paddy, slapping at the ground as he backed off into the sheltered confines of the draw, 'but it sure has put us well and truly on the owl-hoot trail. As from last night, we're both on the dodge.'

'You saddlin' me with the blame for this mess?'

The blunt accusation caught Paddy off guard. He eyed his brother warily.

'You know I didn't mean it that way,' he said stiffly, hands on hips. 'Just statin' the facts, that's all. And the truth is we're now operatin' outside the law.'

'If I could do something about it, don't you think I would?' Finn's tone had turned decidedly chilly.

'Maybe. But you oughtn't to have lit out in such an all-fired hurry in the first place,' countered Paddy, feeling the blood rush to his head. 'All it's done is git Polecat gunned down and the two of us facin' a rope's end.' Paddy was stoked up, and that spelt trouble. 'All I know is it was a durned stupid idea to camp on that claim with a dead man for company.'

'You callin' me a fool, kid?'

'Why not? Any dude worth his salt would have lit out double quick. But not the great Finbar McCall. Ma allus favoured you – her favourite.' The rough timbre of Paddy's voice had risen an octave, his face was flushed with indignation. He aimed a gob of spit at his brother's feet. 'And I ain't no kid!'

'Then don't act like one.'

Paddy clenched his fists, the nails biting deep as Finn continued, his reply equally laced with venom, 'You're just talkin' hogwash. Figure you could have done any better?'

'I sure as hell couldn't have done any worse.'

Normally cool as a mountain stream, Finn had swallowed his pride for long enough. His usually placid features contorted in anger. Without warning he aimed a solid left hook at his brother's jaw.

Caught off guard, Paddy staggered back and tripped

over a rock, sprawling in the dust. But he was a tough kid and on his feet in a trice. He dabbed a finger at the warm trickle of crimson staining his lip. An ugly sneer, menacing and cold, suffused his visage.

'You oughtn't to have done that.' He glowered, hunching his shoulders and squaring off, just like those desperadoes in the comic books. His right hand dropped to the butt of the Colt on his hip.

Then he hesitated. The colour drained from his face. What was he doing? This was no comic strip. This was real life. Paddy suddenly realized what could have happened had he drawn the gun. The stiff back sagged. Curled hands like eagle-talons slumped to his sides. And just like a desert wind, the anger faded and died.

Paddy's head drooped. 'I could have killed you. My own brother.' Tears welled in his eyes.

Finn placed a comforting arm around Paddy's shoulders.

'No you couldn't,' he said quietly.

For ten minutes they just stood, holding on to each other, all the trauma of the last few days erupting to the surface. For the moment, the gravity of their situation was forgotten. They were just two brothers who had rediscovered each other.

It was the cawing of a lone buzzard that eventually broke the spell.

Finn gently pulled away. But there was a fierce glint in his eye.

'I never killed that old guy,' he averred vehemently, 'but if it's the last thing I do, I'll catch the runt what did. Some day, when this ruckus has died down,' he continued with conviction, 'I'll come back and clear my name. But first we need to put some distance between us and the hangman's noose.'

Paddy nodded his head vigorously in agreement.

Sometime around mid-morning, the two brothers were keeping their horses to a gentle trot along the base of a fractured wall of red buttressing. Even with the greater distance from Telluride, they cast frequent glances to their rear, eagle eyes anxiously scanning the rolling terrain for signs of pursuit.

Nothing so far.

Huge flakes of riven sandstone thrust upwards out of the wide basin, with oceans of broken scree fanning out from the towering cliffs. Juniper and sagebrush hugged the side of the trail, their desiccated roots sucking up every last vestige of moisture from the parched ground.

Another hour found them at the entrance to a steep-sided canyon breaking right from the main trail. This must be the San Miguel cut-off through the Chavez Range, surmised Finn. Polecat Wilson had claimed it was dry as a temperance hall but would save them a good five days' travel. Finn's intention was to claim the inheritance left by his father, then sell to the highest bidder before quitting the state. He would mail the proceeds back to his mother.

He reined his mount to a halt and studied the layout at the entrance to the canyon. A faint track led off through a thick belt of rough sagebrush and juniper.

'We'll fill up the canteens from that creek back aways,' he said absently, swinging the chestnut round. But his brother was looking elsewhere. His keen gaze was fixed on a low rise 200 yards downtrail.

'What is it?' from Finn.

Paddy pointed to a plume of grey smoke drifting above the clump of rocks.

'What d'you reckon?'

'Could be a camp-fire,' offered Finn, a note of anxiety in his voice. 'Maybe the posse overtook us during the night.'

'A camp-fire wouldn't create that much smoke,' countered Paddy, screwing his eyes against the sun's glare. 'Could be somebody's in trouble.'

Finn grunted. The last thing he wanted now was getting mixed up in other folk's problems. Paddy sensed his brother's diffidence. But it wasn't in the lad's nature to back off when it came to a showdown.

'We can't just turn away.' Paddy's appeal contained a measure of insistence, his feisty temper lurching to the fore once again. 'Somebody might need our help.' He angled an accusatory glare at his brother. 'And if you won't help, I'll go it alone.'

Finn's sigh contained its own degree of exasperation. Here we go again, he thought.

'All right, all right,' he said, reining his mount towards the source of the smoke. 'But I'll take the lead.' He looked to his brother for agreement. 'And no heroics, *comprendes*?'

Paddy nodded, a thin smile lighting up his boyish face.

Spurring forward towards the rise, they pulled up and dismounted behind a sheltering cluster of rocks, tethered the horses to a yucca, and crept silently to the upper lip of the overhang. Removing his hat, Finn peered over the crest and down into a dried up arroyo. What he saw brought a lump to his throat.

'What can you see?' whispered Paddy edgily, hugging

the bare rock to his rear.

Finn's reaction was to draw his pistol. Trouble with a capital T was obviously brewing. He gestured for his brother to join him on the flat crown of rock.

ELEVEN

RESCUE

About one hundred feet below on the far side of the arroyo, an abandoned buggy burned fiercely. In the breeze fanned by the conflagration, a blue sunshade was desperately attempting to shake off the obdurate flames rapidly devouring it. Still in the traces, a black stallion lay still, a pool of red staining the arroyo, the result of a fatal bullet wound to the head. Hungry buzzards circled overhead attracted by the smell of blood and the prospect of a decent meal for a change.

But it was the action immediately below their place of concealment that drew the attention of the fugitives. A young woman, her clothes in disarray, was struggling desperately in the grip of two shabby individuals. Titian hair flew in all directions as she attempted to shake them off. A futile endeavour heightened by pure terror.

These guys had other things besides plain highway robbery in mind.

Momentarily stunned, the watchers gazed down on the

bizarre scene. The larger of the thugs was holding the girl round the waist whilst his partner tugged at her white blouse half of which had already been torn away revealing the pale skin beneath. It was the ragged tearing of cloth and the accompanying scream that re-energized the brothers. That and the sight of the smaller rat-faced guy unfastening the belt of his pants. The dribbling leer brought a fresh yell of terror from the distraught girl.

'Help! Somebody help me!' The petrified scream was purely instinctive. She had no expectation of some guardian angel descending from the heavens to whisk her away to safety. The passionate entreaty was instantly snatched away by the rising wind.

Her attackers sniggered.

'Nobody round here to save you, girlie.' The thin weasel grinned maliciously. His black moustache quivered with lurid anticipation.

'Bastards!' The distraught epithet spewed from Finn's taut lips.

Only spawn of the devil resorted to such means to assuage their carnal desires. The average frontiersman, stoical and hard-working, baulked at the very thought of mistreating women.

'We gotta do something,' sang out Paddy slithering down from their place of concealment. 'Them skunks are gonna. . . .' he spluttered, unable to bring himself to mouth the abominable words.

'Don't I know it,' replied Finn, his eyes blazing. He followed closely on Paddy's heels, sweat beading his worried features. Alarm at what the girl was being subjected to spurred the intrepid rescuers onward. Scuttling round the side of the untidy rock cluster, they shunted down a narrow scree-choked gully. The noisy rattle of stones, along with sharp thorn bushes grabbing at their coats, were ignored in the headlong dash to save the girl.

At the bottom, Paddy came to a sudden halt. The girl was splayed out on the ground, the two bushwhackers standing over her. Rat-face had his pants down exposing dirty pink long johns. Luckily their backs were turned. Finn signalled for his brother to circle behind whilst he challenged them head on. There was no time to lose.

And that was the precise moment the girl eyeballed her liberators.

Large orbs popping, her frightened gaze was momentarily diverted from the hideous treatment being meted out. Rat-face immediately discerned the change in his victim's manner. Even with his lascivious desires straining at the leash, he knew something was amiss. And that could only mean one thing.

He paused, eyes shiftily flicking to the right. A dark shadow drifted across his vision. Larger than any animal, it had to be an intruder. He cursed silently. His gun had been tossed aside in the heat of the moment. There it was, six feet to his left, half buried in sand.

A snarl as if from some rabid beast erupted from the guy's ugly slit of a mouth. Quick as a striking rattler, he threw himself sideways. Snatching at the ancient Colt Dragoon, he fanned the hammer, swivelled and fired. The shot sang past Finn's ear. Glancing off a rock, it ricocheted away with the whine of an angry hornet.

Finn returned the fire. But he had been taken by surprise and his own shots failed to hit their target. The assailant was now on his feet, hauling back on the old revolver's stiff hammer for another shot. His bestial face registered panic. This would be his last chance.

In that brief instant of time, as he held the brute's gaze, Finn recognized that same weasely sneer, the cold merciless eyes.

The Flagg twins!

The very same who had been in the posse that arrested him. They had been all for stringing him up there and then.

That fluttering recall stayed Finn's trigger finger. Only for the briefest of instants but enough for Amos Flagg. His gun spat flame, the deadly blast punching Finn backwards.

'Aaaaaaagh!' A choked yelp was wrenched from his throat. Lurching back a pace, he clutched at his injured left shoulder, his face creased in pain. The bushwhacker mouthed an evil snarl of triumph, aiming the gun for the final denouement. His finger tightened on the trigger.

Finn stared death in the face – and the reaper bade him welcome.

But his time had not yet come. Two shots erupted from his right. Both found their mark, the first catching the snake full in the centre of his chest, the second blowing away half his face. Blood and treacle splattered across the dull orange hardpan of the arroyo. High above, the circling predators squawked their appreciation.

On this occasion, Paddy McCall uttered a grunt of satisfaction. This killing he had enjoyed. And the contents of his stomach remained steady. Finn breathed a sigh of relief at his brother's timely intervention, more than grateful for the hours of shooting practice the youngster had put in back on the farm. Blue smoke drifted from the short barrel of the Peacemaker as it shifted towards the hulking bruiser still holding the girl in a grip of steel.

Caleb Flagg looked aghast. But he was sufficiently alert to keep the tip of a deadly Bowie knife prodding the white skin of her swanlike neck. Terror suffused the poor girl's waxen features.

'Come one step closer,' growled Flagg, tickling the girl's throat, 'and I'll spill her guts in the sand.' Piggy eyes, glazed with hate, lanced the two rescuers as he inched towards the horses tethered nearby. 'I aim to ride outa here with the girl as hostage. You know what'll happen if'n you try to follow.' He took another step towards the mounts. 'Now spin that hardware into them rocks yonder.'

Paddy stood his ground, crouched in the classic gunfighter's stance, gun barrel wavering.

'You heard me!' rasped Flagg, emphasizing his demand with a flick of the lethal blade. Blood trickled from a small cut. The girl shrieked, more through sheer panic than anything else. It was enough to show her saviours that Caleb Flagg meant business. The guns disappeared into the rocks.

Finn was helpless, impotent. He was aware that something had to be done if the girl was to be saved. And soon. No matter what the bastard said now, Flagg would have to kill her at some point so she couldn't identify him.

Stall for time. Keep him talking. Once the skunk was mounted and away, anything could happen.

'Remember me, do you, Caleb?'

The hulk paused. 'How d'you know me?' he demanded.

'You were in the posse at Dirty Devil Creek investigatin' the murder of the old prospector.'

Caleb's brain was slow to catch on. His ugly mug formed a perplexed squint.

Finn nudged the laggard brain. 'I was the one you arrested.'

Brooding eyes popped as the penny dropped.

'You oughta be in jail,' Caleb croaked.

'I escaped.' Finn smirked sensing that their fortunes were about to change, 'thanks to the assistance of my partner here.' He slung a thumb towards his brother, offering him a wry wink. 'Recognize the hangman, do you?'

Flagg was nonplussed, baffled. Such bizarre happenings were beyond the workings of a dim-witted mind. Without Amos to guide him, the simpleton allowed his guard to fall. As the burly grip slackened around her body, the girl sucked in a deep breath, raised her leg and brought the heel of her boot down sharply on the clumsy oaf's foot.

An agonized croak spewed from the gaping orifice below his straggly moustache. He let out a choking gasp of pain but still managed to retain a hold on the girl. Knowing this was her last opportunity, Sarah girded herself and stamped down again twice in quick succession.

This time he let go sufficiently for her to squirm beneath the encircling clasp. One almighty heave and Flagg reeled away drunkenly.

'Get him!' yelled Finn.

Paddy didn't need any urging. He sprinted across the intervening ten yards. Somewhat out of character, Caleb Flagg had recovered quickly. He faced the oncoming lunge, the demonic smile as lethal as the blade reflecting the overhead sun. Half bent, Paddy scooped up a handful of sand and threw it into Flagg's ugly face.

Then he was upon the burly miner. Grabbing the knife hand, he strove ineffectually to loosen the brute's hold. Staggering across the width of the arroyo they grappled, a

110

pair of demented ballet dancers giving the performance of a lifetime.

But Flagg was too powerful. Simple he might be, but not when it came to fighting. Like a mad bull, he spewed out a rabid snarl, flipping the lean youngster on to his back, all his weight forcing down on to the knife. Veins stood out on Paddy's blotchy neck as he strained to prevent the fatal cutting edge from slicing him open. Sheer panic lent impetus to his sapping energy. The wicked point edged closer to his throat. But the herculean strength of the giant was too much.

'Use your knees to break his hold!'

Through the misty haze, Finn's strident call went unheeded. Paddy knew his end was nigh. He hadn't the strength to continue the one-sided conflict. Hot breath rasped harshly in his throat.

When all seemed lost, the raging bear was suddenly flung aside, snatched by the hand of some unseen Goliath. The knife spun away. Without waiting to determine the source of his good fortune, Paddy grabbed the handle, flung himself on to the recumbent body and buried eight inches of shiny steel into the bulging chest. Three times he tore the razored edge from the bloodied torso, stabbing frenziedly.

Only the intercession of a calm lilting voice finally brought a cessation to the frenetic attack, dragging him back from the brink.

Flapping wings overhead sounded like applause.

'I think he's dead now.' Firm, insistent hands drew the lad to his feet and guided him away from the carnage. Having thrown aside the hefty branch she had so effectively used to club her assailant, the girl then sat Paddy down, his back resting against a chunk of sandstone. She wetted a cloth and gently wiped his dazed face.

'Well done, Paddy,' Finn said. Then to the girl, 'And to you, miss. It was us who were supposed to be the rescuers. Not the other way round.' His laugh had a hollow ring. The girl flushed, pulling her torn blouse around slim shoulders.

'I don't know how to thank you, gentlemen,' she averred ardently. 'If you hadn't come along when you did, I hate to imagine what the consequences would have been.' Her head dropped at the thought, tears of joy and relief trickling down her smooth cheeks. Looking up, her eye was drawn to Finn's blood-soaked shirtsleeve, then to the warped expression on his face. A shocked gasp escaped from lips that were the prettiest Finn had ever seen. This man clearly needed her help.

'You've been shot!' she exclaimed.

'Just a flesh wound,' he muttered affecting a nonchalant air.

'Nonsense!' replied the girl, flicking back her long hair, 'I'm a nurse. And I can't have one of my knights errant bleeding to death.' Luckily her bag of tricks had been thrown clear when the buggy crashed out of control after the horse was shot dead.

Finn's injury was soon expertly dressed. He held out his good hand.

'Finbar McCall of Plaintree, Kansas,' he said, accepting a welcome drink from the girl's canteen. 'And this is my young brother Patrick.'

'That's Paddy, ma'am' interrupted the younger man. 'Nobody calls me Patrick, 'ceptin' on Sundays at church.'

The girl smiled. A radiant aura bathed her serene face.

Bright hazel eyes glimmered like jewels in a crown. Both men stared open-mouthed.

'My name is Nurse Sarah Tindle,' she responded lightly, having recovered quickly from her ordeal.

Instantly the two men stiffened. Sarah caught their mood.

'What is it?' she asked eyeing the pair with a baffled frown. 'Is there something wrong?'

Finn shuffled uncomfortably. Paddy felt distinctly awkward.

It was Finn who finally spoke up, nervously playing with the brim of his hat.

'Might you be the daughter of Ezra Tindle, a gold prospector from down Missouri way?'

'The very same.' A worried quaver had crept into her hesitant response. 'How do you know my father?'

'I'm sorry,' he began choking on his words, 'but we have some bad news.'

Her shoulders slumped, tears welled in her large eyes. She looked from one to the other, but they were unable to meet her fervent gaze.

'He's dead, isn't he?' The tone was flat, devoid of feeling. Almost as if she'd expected the revelation. 'How did it happen?'

Paddy eyed his brother askance.

Finn coughed. Then he related the train of events that had brought them together in this remote backwater of south-west Colorado. He surmised that the Flaggs, being down-at-heel gold-panners, had probably reckoned that waylaying solitary travellers would pay better. They had figured wrong.

In the main Sarah kept her peace, listening, absorbing

the grim tidings. An inscrutable expression revealed nothing of what she clearly felt beneath the hard shell. Interjecting at suitable points, Paddy added his own bizarre experience in the guise of a hangman. Only then did the impenetrable mask slip, an amused smile playing across the satin contours of her face.

'So what is the daughter of a prospector doing in this wilderness?' enquired Finn, clearly intrigued by this handsome female. 'And travellin' alone.' It was evident that Sarah Tindle possessed an independence of spirit normally only associated with church matriarchs.

Studying the two brothers, Sarah felt deep within her soul that she could trust them. And now she was going to require help in her quest to avenge her father's killing.

She then went on to explain how Ezra had written to her about a map he had drawn indicating the hiding-place of the mammoth gold nugget.

'He couldn't trust his partner,' she went on. 'Figured he might pull a stunt like this. That's why he lodged the map with an attorney in Telluride. A man called Jack Brubekker.'

Finn perked up his ears.

'*Dandy* Jack Brubekker.' The name elicited a caustic snort of derision. 'He was the prosecutin' lawyer what found me guilty of killin' your pa. A scheming toad who bent everything I had to say in my defence.' Finn was seething. 'He would have watched me swing if it hadn't been for Paddy and his new-found career.'

'It's my good fortune you didn't,' replied Sarah before continuing with her story. 'Dad always wrote to me regularly every month. Never missed. So when a couple of months went by with no letter, I got to being worried. And here I am.'

Then Paddy asked, 'What are your plans now, miss?'

'I think after all we've been through together, you can call me Sarah.' The girl smiled coyly.

'Sure thing, Miss . . . Sarah.'

They all laughed to ease the tension.

'Its my aim to travel on to Telluride and pay this Dandy Jack Brubekker a visit.'

'I seem to remember while I was sweatin' it out in the hoosegow,' said Finn slowly, 'the sheriff mentioned that Brubekker hadn't been seen around town since the trial ended. Nor Curly Joe Deakin, the skunk who I'm certain is the real killer.'

Sarah gave an understanding nod. 'Dad described him to me in his last letter. Called him a layabout who didn't pull his weight on the claim,' interrupted Sarah quickly, 'He suspected something like this might happen.'

Paddy scratched his head in thought.

'That lawyer sounds like a real slippery cuss to me. A fast-talkin' dude like that wouldn't think twice about featherin' his own nest.' He had been helping the girl to sort out those belongings that had survived the conflagration. The small buggy had burnt itself out. It was now little more than a blackened shell. Threads of smoke filtered from the ashes. 'I figure that pair of double-dealin' coyotes have stolen the map and gone into the gold-huntin' business on their own account.'

Finn agreed, sighing heavily. 'But we have no idea which way they might have gone.'

'Could be anyplace by now.'

'Other side of the moon, even.'

'That's where you're wrong,' avowed Sarah butting in on their disconsolate reveries.

Both men stared at her vacantly.

'I have my own copy of the map stating exactly where the nugget is hidden.' Sarah grinned and delved into her carpetbag which had fortunately escaped the blaze. 'Dad sent me one just in case.' She impishly tapped her aquiline nose.

'Seems like the old guy had more marbles than folks gave him credit for,' said Finn.

'I also bought a state map of Colorado from the land registry office when I passed through Cortez,' added the girl, unfolding the two items and laying them out on the ground.

'Maybe now we can put the kibosh on them no good varmints,' blurted an eager Paddy McCall.

'And then I can clear my name.' Finn's response was more deliberate. He still had a murder charge hanging over him. But it didn't stop him peering wide-eyed at the all-important chart, avidly devouring the black spidery drawings. After a brief scan, he stabbed a grubby finger at a cross.

'Black Canyon!' he exclaimed curtly. 'Polecat Wilson reckoned it's the wildest spot on earth. Only the toughest mountain men ever stray in there.'

'Just the sort of remote wilderness to hide a priceless gold nugget,' responded Paddy.

For a full minute, all three stared at the chart, roughly scratched with a blunt quill, but accurate nonetheless. It was Sarah who broke the silence.

'I still intend going on to Telluride.' The declaration was firm, decisive. 'I need to be sure that this lawyer Jack

Brubekker really has stolen the map. And maybe I can find out when they actually left the town.'

'Are you certain this is what you want to do?' asked Finn.

The girl held his gaze with a brief nod.

The brothers could see that her mind was made up.

'You'll have to accompany Sarah,' Finn said to his brother, wincing as the painful throbbing in his shoulder returned. 'Make camp in the foothills overlooking Telluride. Only go in if Sarah gets herself in bother,' he advised, offering a warm handshake. 'I'll expect you back here by noon tomorrow. No later.'

Sarah kissed him lightly on the cheek. The unexpected touch sent shivers through his body. This was one female he definitely wanted to see again. After Paddy had retrieved their horses from behind the rocks and located their guns, the young farmer and the nurse mounted up. A brisk salute from Paddy, a look of affection from Sarah and they were gone.

Finn struggled to his feet, his intention being to make his own camp in what shade he could find out of the searing heat. It was already past noon. The sun was striking down on the exposed arroyo with all its blatant power, greedily sucking at the arid sand. This was no place for a wounded man.

TWELVE

REVENGE

It was the smell that informed Paddy they were approaching Telluride. A mixture of unwashed bodies, rotting vegetation and human waste. Sarah wrinkled her nose.

'They say you soon get used to it.' Paddy smirked, reining in his chestnut mare.

'Well, the quicker I find out the truth, the sooner we can leave,' she responded acidly.

'I'll camp in this draw off the trail. Brubekker's office is a block east of the jailhouse.' A devious smile creased Paddy's face. 'I wonder if they've blocked up the hole we left.'

Without replying, Sarah nudged her horse down the constricted draw and back on to the main trail.

'Now you be careful,' Paddy called after her retreating back. She waved an acknowledgement and spurred to a gentle trot. She entered the outskirts of the town from the west. So this was the rip-roaring hell's kitchen they called Telluride. A far cry from the urbane life style she had enjoyed back in Sacramento. And people actually chose to live here.

The sun had already slipped below the western horizon. What little luminosity persisted had thrown the untidy huddle of buildings into shadowy relief. It enabled her to pass unnoticed down the main street. Her long hair was pinned up beneath her wide-brimmed Stetson, her shoulders hunkered into a corduroy topcoat. Just another gold-hungry adventurer come to seek his fortune. Only the eyes gave her away. Tense and apprehensive, they flickered about, nervously scanning the sidewalks.

A signboard nailed to the only stone building in sight drew her gaze. On it printed in red was the immortal legend she was after: *Sheriff's Office.* A quick glance up and down the street, then she steered the horse over to the hitching post outside. After tying up, she knocked on the heavy oak door. A muffled voice laced with impatience bade her enter, but only after a second, more insistent rap.

Jake Montane was sitting at his desk, a forkful of apple pie stuck in his mouth. Sarah sniffed disdainfully. Not exactly the warmest of welcomes. This guy obviously resented having his supper interrupted. She stood by the door, waiting. After some moments the sheriff pushed back his chair, came round the desk and poured himself a mug of hot coffee from a pot simmering on the pot-bellied stove. Dark, hooded eyes, oozing mistrust, never left the girl's face. He was figuring that from now on he would lock the door at meal times. Too many interruptions.

'Well, what d'you want, mister?' The question was more like an order, spat out with derision. No wonder Finn McCall had been railroaded with a bogus charge if this misfit was the only law around.

She smiled inwardly at the lawdog's gender misconception, but kept her thoughts well hidden, her face a stony mask of indifference. From the battered hat down to the faded Levis and muddy boots, Sarah Tindle's disguise was complete. Only when she spoke was the illusion dispelled.

'I'm looking for a lawyer by the name of Brubekker,' she said firmly, taking off her hat to reveal the smooth, rather elfin features of a more than pretty female. She pouted demurely to enhance the effect, long legs splayed apart, hands on hips. The tactics worked.

Montane almost dropped his coffee mug. He stammered out an embarrassed response.

'Errrm, s-sorry, miss. I figured you wus one of them no-account miners come pesterin' me.' Quickly remembering his manners, he offered her a chair, solicitously dusting the seat with the cloth from his supper tray. 'Can I git you a coffee?'

'No, thank you,' she replied quietly, hands firmly clasped on her lap. Outwardly calm and in control, Sarah felt decidedly queasy, her insides a screwed-up mess. Large doelike eyes peered up at him endearingly. 'You haven't answered my question, Sheriff.'

Montane swallowed hard.

'Dandy Jack!' He muttered the name in a disparaging tone whilst wiping the crumbs from his mouth. 'He quit town soon after officiatin' at the murder trial of a claim-jumper. It appears like he left in a hurry, too.'

'Is the murderer here now?' enquired Sarah innocently.

'No, he ain't,' snapped back Montane. 'Some damn blasted accomplice impersonated the state hangman then busted him out of the cell. Pardon my language, miss,' he apologized with a quick bow of his grizzly pate.

'Have you any idea which direction they took?' she said, trying not to appear too inquisitive.

'They hired a buckboard and headed west. But the trail disappeared into thin air. I've had men scouring the whole of the park. Not a sign of the varmints.' Montane gave a shake of his head. 'Some mighty strange goin's-on around this here town recently,' he reflected, slurping his coffee.

Sarah offered him a suitably puzzled lift of the eyebrows.

'You were saying about this lawyer.'

'Erm,' continued the lawman. 'The dude jumped in on a dangerous fracas what had blown up in the Silver Dollar saloon. Saved the old prospector's partner from a serious lickin'. Rainbow Pincher, the barman, said they left the saloon together after the fight. Next thing, the pair of 'em have hightailed it.' He clicked his fingers. 'Vanished into thin air.' He shook his head, visibly unsettled. 'And another thing,' he went on quickly, 'The saloon deadbeat, a drunk called Jackdaw Lassiter, has also gone missin'.' Montane paced the office, then threw up his arms in despair. 'I figured this job fer an easy ride when I took it. Now I ain't so sure.'

Having discovered all she was able from the baffled lawman, Sarah thanked him and stood up to leave.

'Did you have business with Brubekker?' he asked as she tugged open the office door.

Sarah was ready with her story. 'I have been left some land,' she stated confidently, 'and Mr Brubekker is holding the authorization papers.'

'So who shall I say is askin' after him?' replied the sheriff, 'that is, if he ever puts in an appearance.'

'The name is Sarah T. . . .' Just in the nick of time she stopped herself.

Montane raised a bushy eyebrow.

'Sarah Turner,' she said, keeping her reply flat and detached.

The sheriff scratched his head. 'Don't reckon I recollect that handle,' he murmured uncertainly.

'Hyram Turner is my uncle,' she hurried on, anxious to bring the meeting to a conclusion and depart. 'An absentee landowner. He rents the land out to local stock breeders.' Not giving the man chance to quiz her further, Sarah quickly changed the subject. 'Is there a hotel in town?'

'Sure thing, miss,' he responded. 'Try the Rodeo Palace down the end of the street. Best in town. In fact it's the only place in Telluride with rooms suitable for a lady.'

Sarah nodded her appreciation. 'Once again, many thanks for your help, Sheriff. No doubt we will be seeing each other again.' The eyelids fluttered.

'I will look forward to it, Miss Turner.'

Sarah Tindle allowed herself a wry smile and was gone.

Soon after daybreak, she rode out of Telluride, ensuring that nobody was following. Satisfied the coast was clear, she reined her mount into the draw where Paddy was waiting all saddled up and ready to go.

'Find out anything useful?' he asked eagerly.

Sarah laughed, feeling pleased with her subterfuge.

'You and your brother certainly upset the apple cart and no mistake. That sheriff's in a right stew.'

After breaking camp, they were soon heading back to join Finn, using a series of back trails to avoid any unwelcome attention.

A low rumbling of shod hoofs caused Finn to scramble to his feet. The Navy cocked and ready, he peeped round the edge of the rocks. He was relieved to see it was his brother and Sarah Tindle. He stepped out from cover and holstered the revolver.

'How you feelin'?' asked Sarah, dismounting quickly to check on Finn's shoulder.

'It still throbs like the devil, but there's no fresh bleedin'.'

After a cursory glance at the dressing, her face split into a radiant smile that turned Finn's legs to jelly.

'You'll live,' she beamed, chirpily assuring him that the wound was clean. A sharp wince hissed from between tight lips as the girl gently probed the wound.

Even though the slug had only creased the skin, it had still ploughed a deep furrow across his shoulder. Not life-threatening, but intensely painful. Luckily Sarah was able to apply a soothing balm that dulled the throbbing ache whilst accelerating the healing process. And with a full day's rest behind him, Finn now felt ready to set out in pursuit of their quarry.

'So what's the action?' He addressed the girl.

'It sure looks like those two thieves have lit out after the gold. The sheriff fell for my story. He's too worried about losing his job to be chasing all over the country looking for us. He hasn't the least notion as to where you disappeared to.'

Finn considered for a moment. 'In that case, I figure once the lousy rats have located the nugget, they'll head fer the nearest main town to sell it.'

'Where will that be?'

'Show me the map again.'

Sarah unfolded the chart on the ground.

Finn stabbed at the chart, almost poking a finger through the heavy paper.

'Purgatory!' he asserted confidently. 'They'll want to find a town with an assay office large enough to pay their price without asking too many awkward questions.'

Utilizing the spare horse as a pack animal, they were soon heading back up the trail. Finn called a halt where the San Miguel cut-off forked north beside a marker cairn. This was the old Indian trail the brothers had almost taken the day before. He dismounted, indicating for his brother to do likewise.

Satisfying the girl's questioning look he said, 'We don't want anybody followin' us. You lead the horses up the trail and wait there.' The brothers then commenced to brush out their tracks with some loose branches.

Inside the defile, daylight was almost excluded. The vertical crack being so narrow, they were forced to ride in single file, saddle-packs scraping the bare rock walls. Within the cramped passage, every sound resonated eerily. As they twisted further and further into the rocky fastness, a sense of unease settled over the three travellers. About 200 feet above, a thin sliver of blue offered a welcome glimpse of that other world, a tantalizing link so near, yet so far. The claustrophobic ravine seemed to go on for ever: a subterranean gallery of oppressive gloom.

'When we likely to reach open country?'

Paddy's hesitant query was in all their minds.

'Not far now,' said Finn, trying to inject a measure of reassurance into his reply even though he had never passed this way before. All he had to guide him were the recollections of his dead partner. As he scanned the smooth red walls, one particular comment made by Polecat Wilson struck him with brute force.

That's Ute country, and them red devils don't take kindly to strangers interferin' with their sacred burial grounds. Maybe we oughta take the long way round.

That's right, Finn reflected to himself. But a reversal of direction was not an option in the constricted defile. So they continued onwards. On either side roughly carved sketches depicting ancient rites of passage into the next life stared back at them, pointing the finger of accusation. In the lead, Finn drew to a halt. A brooding atmosphere of death hung over the ravine. The silence was almost tangible, heavy with menace. Even the horses appeared to sense the sombre mood, white froth bubbling from flared nostrils.

Sarah shivered involuntarily. Paddy glanced nervously at his brother.

Ute tribal law decreed that violators of this hallowed place should be punished. Perhaps the travellers had somehow recognized this?

Time missed a beat as they waited for Finn to lead off.

Then it happened.

A fine mist of red dust drifted down from the heights above. Finn looked up. What he saw was from the pages of some horror comic. Black wriggling tentacles filled the narrow void. Hissing and writhing they plunged towards the interlopers accompanied by a spine-chilling howl of fury.

The Ute revenge.

For the briefest of instants, Finn remained immobile, rigid as a temperance dame. Fear of what a basketful of rattlers could achieve in the confined space of the ravine broke the hypnotic spell.

'Ride, you sons-of-the-saddle!' he yelled jabbing steel-rowelled spurs into his horse's flanks. 'Ride like the hounds of hell are on yer tail.' Without any second invitation, the three horses lunged forward equally encouraged by their riders. Heads bent low, leathers slapping furiously, pounding hoofs drummed on the canyon floor. The raucous din resonated fearfully between the enclosed walls like a tribal war dance.

One of the writhing monsters struck Finn on the head. Whipping his hat off, he fended it away, the snapping fangs inches from his sweating face. Behind him, a full-grown diamond-back slapped against Paddy's outstretched arms, burying its lethal poison-packers into the saddle horn. In his haste to dislodge the venomous reptile, the Hawken he had been carrying vanished into the murky haze of the ravine. The loss of his trusted weapon was of secondary importance in their current predicament. Grabbing the thick scaly body, the young man prised the deadly jaws open and smashed the ogre's flat head against the rock wall as it flashed by.

In what seemed like a blink in time, the headlong flight brought the travellers out into open country. Thankfully they had all escaped unscathed due primarily to Finn's hawk-eyed observation. All, that was, except for one casualty.

The pack-horse at the rear had borne the brunt of the attack. Trailing third in line, Sarah had dropped the lead rope when the mad dash for safety was called. Not so astute, the horse had found itself facing off a dozen sets of lungeing fangs. It hadn't stood a chance. Struggling gamely onward for a few more paces, its front legs had finally crumpled as the poison coursed through the trembling frame.

The grateful trio reined up and looked back to the narrow fissure they had recently vacated. The pack-animal lay in a crumpled heap, the ugly black creatures squirming and thrashing around their prey.

Sarah drew their attention to the serrated rim of the sandstone canyon. A thin line of figures stood on the edge, unmoving like statues, peering down at their quarry. Each set of antagonists held the other's gaze, neither seeming to want to break the stillness of the moment. It was Finn who made the first move, gently nudging his mount along the base of the canyon.

'It seems like the contest is over,' he murmured ruefully, maintaining a steady gaze on the stony figures. 'Remind me not to return by this route.' The harsh guffaw sounded hollow in the confines of the ravine.

Another two hours and they had entered a more rolling terrain broken up with deep gullies and sprinkled with cactus and yucca. It was an empty, dry land with nothing to attract permanent settlement except that of the red man. Thankfully the Ute appeared satisfied that their resting forebears had been amply recompensed for the ill-fated incursion. To the north, a line of rising buttes and mesas indicated to Finn that they were nearing their destination.

The trail now dropped steeply in a series of steep zigzags across the face of an elongated mesa. Extreme care was needed on the loose, stony descent, which prompted Finn to instruct the others to dismount and walk their horses down to the broad amphitheatre below. A level plain cut by numerous dry gullies stretched for about ten miles with a similar wall of red at the far side. His eyes crinkled to thin slits. At this distance it appeared impenetrable. But there had to be a way through.

Polecat Wilson had found it. So would he.

At the bottom of the cliff, Finn spotted a trickle of water seeping from some deep underground source. A mere drop in an ocean of sand, it was like an oasis to the parched riders. As the shadows were lengthening towards dusk, he called a halt. Camping in the bed of an arroyo could be dangerous at this time of year when run-off from the high country was apt to change the landscape overnight, swelling the dry beds into raging torrents. But tiredness and Finn's weakened condition removed any degree of choice in the matter.

'We'll camp here for the night,' he said. 'Tomorrow should see us in Purgatory around noon if we make an early start.'

THIRTEEN

PURGATORY

As they crested a low rise, the two riders saw their destination nestling in the valley bottom within a huge meander of the Gunnison River. Enclosing it on all sides, towering pinnacles thrust their jagged snouts at the blue sky, each vying for centre stage. The town appeared to exude an air of prosperity set amidst the verdant sward. This was clearly rich cattle country with numerous longhorn steers mingling with imported Herefords.

Although Purgatory had grown up on a diet of beef, recent gold strikes in the surrounding high country had turned it into a burgeoning local centre for the sale of the precious metal. Being a new contender in the commercial game would ensure the best price was paid. Dandy Jack smiled. The town also lay off the main trails heading west, which would greatly assist their disappearance once the transaction was completed.

This was the reason Brubekker had persuaded his

young partner that Purgatory was the best place for selling the nugget.

'Remember what we agreed,' the lawyer reminded Deakin as they surveyed the growing settlement. 'I'll take charge of the nugget from here and deposit it with the assay agent. He'll need to weigh it and calculate its value before settling on a price.'

The kid was edgy. He didn't cotton to parting with his loot. By this time, he'd hoped to have disposed of the tricky dude in Black Canyon. His figuring hadn't run to sharing out the proceeds. But Brubekker was a devious customer, and he needed the lawyer for the negotiations regarding the sale of their ill-gotten gains. Although Deakin would never own to the fact, he was a simple country hick lacking the necessary skills when it came to the cut and thrust of commercial transactions. Brubekker knew this and had played on it.

'You go into the nearest saloon and wait for me,' he said, adding tersely, 'and don't drink too much. Any loose talk could spell disaster.'

Deakin grunted unenthusiastically, then spurred his horse forward down the low grade, followed closely by Brubekker. A sly smirk creased the lawyer's oily features as he caressed the bag containing the priceless nugget. He had every intention of coming out of this the winner.

As they entered the outskirts of the town, it was obvious that Purgatory was going places. All the buildings were painted different colours. Even the main street had a name. Emblazoned in black on a white background, a printed sign affixed to the side of the livery barn read *Gunnison Avenue*. The local council had even gone to the lengths of planting imported poplars on either side.

Deakin nodded thoughtfully. There was money here. Brubekker had chosen well. This place was most definitely no Telluride.

He climbed off his horse in front of the first saloon, a prosperous establishment boasting the epithet *Roscoe's Roundup* in gold lettering. He hitched up and entered the smoky interior leaving Brubekker to continue down the street in search of the assay office. He sauntered up to the polished mahogany bar and ordered a beer. Two other drinkers stood at the bar, boots resting idly on the brass footrail. Hunched over their drinks, the pair ignored the youthful stranger. In frontier settlements, minding your own business was the healthier option. Especially when a newcomer sported a gleaming low-slung six-shooter.

The bartender was different. After all, it was his job to be friendly.

'Come far, stranger?' he asked, sliding a foaming glass across the shiny surface.

Deakin eyed him casually, took a long slurp then belched loudly.

'Some,' he mumbled incoherently.

'Staying long?' persisted the jovial barkeep.

'Maybe. Then maybe not.'

'Looking for work?'

Deakin's brow knitted, his expression tightening. But he remained silent, slaking his thirst once again.

'There's plenty of ranches in the valley taking on hands,' offered the man, unaware that he was breaking the unwritten law.

Was the guy a tenderfoot, or just ignorant? Deakin didn't ask. He slammed the pot down hard, grabbed the unsuspecting guy and half-dragged him over the bartop, his lurid face almost touching the other's.

The kid's reaction stunned the bartender. A cold sweat blistered his flushed visage.

'All I came in here for was a quiet drink, not to have some nosy turnip givin' me the shakedown. Got the message?'

The barman gave a quaking nod. Deakin flung him back, then carried on as if nothing had happened. The two locals hunkered deeper into their coats, sidling away from the young rannie.

When Brubekker arrived, the assay office was empty of customers. He smiled confidently on entering. Behind the counter a small dapper individual with slicked down black hair was filling out a form.

'Be with you in a second,' he said without looking up.

When Brubekker had removed the gold nugget from its oilskin wrapping, he placed it in front of the clerk. Still the man kept to his task.

'I have something here you might be interested in.' The lawyer could barely keep the excitement from his voice.

Pushing aside the forms, the little man peered haughtily at his visitor.

'You have something to sell?' His tone was arrogant, curt, as though he was more used to dealing with low-life miners offering tiny pokes. Brubekker's eyes dropped to the object squatting on the counter. The clerk's piggy eyes almost popped out of his head. For a full minute, words failed him as he stared, gob-smacked at the largest gold nugget he had ever seen.

At last he croaked, 'I'll have to wire head office in Durango about this.'

Brubekker chuckled inwardly, enjoying the pen-pusher's confusion.

'You do that,' he said, putting his signature to the deed of authorization absently pushed at him by the astounded agent.Once he had seen the nugget locked away in a large wall safe, he asked the man where he could find a room. 'I'll be staying in town for a few days . . .' He paused while the agent countersigned the holding document. '. . . until I decide whether to accept your offer.'

The agent huffed and fluttered around like a squawking parrot. His tight collar was throttling him. If he let something like this escape, the bossman in Durango would skin him alive.

'I am sure the company will be more than pleased to meet your requirements, sir.' The little weasel was fawning, his syrupy vocals ingratiating.

'So which is the best hotel?' Brubekker's eyes lifted as if he expected nothing less.

'The Ranch House at the end of North Street is the best in town,' replied the smarmy agent, rubbing his damp hands. 'Tell the manager that Harvey Wallstock recommended you stay there.'

'Thank you, Mr Wallstock,' Dandy Jack straightened his necktie. 'I will await your call.'

'You can depend on it, sir.'

The little toady even bowed him out of the door. On leaving the assay office, the lawyer couldn't resist a merry chortle as he strolled down towards North Street. This was going better than he could ever have anticipated.

The Ranch House was an impressive wooden building painted brown with a veranda running all the way around the second storey. He booked two adjacent rooms for himself and his partner, informing the desk clerk that he would likely be staying three days at the most. It was Jack's intention to have a wash, then change into some clean duds before going to join his partner.

Unfortunately, the tiring journey from Black Canyon had taken its toll. That and the constant strain of keeping watch on the kid. Flopping down on to the soft mattress of the double bed, a total weariness enveloped his exhausted frame. Within a minute he was fast asleep, dead to the world. A gentle snore stirred the fleshy lips.

Some twenty minutes later Paddy McCall jigged his mount along Gunnison Avenue. He was impressed. Purgatory was the first town he had visited aspiring to a church with its own clock tower. He drew rein outside Roscoe's Roundup and pushed open the batwings. Only a handful of customers were at the bar. Ordering himself a beer, Paddy frowned at the surly bartender. A friendly word didn't cost anything. He let it pass and moved away to a table. Feller probably woke up with a sore head.

Finn and Sarah arrived together in Gunnison Avenue some ten minutes later.

'Keep your eyes peeled,' urged the girl, knowing that only Finn would be able to recognize the two robbers. Finn's lean face hardened as he scanned the street, unimpressed for the time being by its obvious prosperity.

Then he noticed Paddy's chestnut outside a saloon. Typical of his younger brother, thought Finn. First priority is a drink. They tied off and mounted the boardwalk. Finn cupped his hands and peered through the window of the saloon.

'Is he there?' enquired Sarah from behind.

Finn tensed, his back stiffening.

'What is it?'

'The guy at the bar,' hissed Finn briskly, indicating a scruffy young rannigan slouching over his drink. 'That's Curly Joe Deakin.'

The other customers were giving him a wide berth. Maybe it had something to do with the conspicuous Schofield on his hip; that and the dark air of menace emanating from him.

'But where's Paddy?' Finn added, anxiously scrutinizing the room. Dust hung in the air, catching the light cast by sunbeams lancing in through the front window. The dazzling effect made it hard to distinguish anything in the deeper recesses. It was Sarah who spotted their young associate.

'Over there by that alcove!' she exclaimed. Paddy was idly playing solitaire completely unaware of the dangerous situation he was in. 'I'm going in to warn him.' Without waiting to judge Finn's reaction, she turned and made for the door. Just in time, Finn pulled her back.

'You can't go in there,' he remonstrated with her earnestly.

'Why not?'

'It just ain't done,' said a rather bemused Finn. 'The only women what go into saloons are dancing girls and those who . . . who—'

'I know,' interrupted Sarah with candour, 'What you're trying to say is women who are soiled doves. Those who sell their bodies.'

Finn's face coloured visibly at the girl's unashamed manner. She really was a type of female he had never encountered before. Maybe she even smoked!

'Just because I live in Sacramento doesn't mean I don't know the ways of the world,' she told him.

Once again she tried to push past him. But Finn was adamant. The West just wasn't ready for independent women yet awhile.

'It ain't just 'cos you're a lady,' he advised cautiously, 'but them guys in there wouldn't take kindly to their den bein' invaded, so to speak. You would attract too much unwanted attention. And it could put Paddy in far more danger than he's in right now.' He estimated her reaction before continuing with a shrug. 'I can't go in. That skunk would recognize me straight away.'

Thankfully the girl appeared to comprehend the logic of this contention.

Finn breathed a sigh of relief, then hurried on: 'I'm wonderin' where that dude Brubekker is hidin' out.' A quick glance up and down both sides of Gunnison Avenue was sufficient to assure him that Dandy Jack was elsewhere.

At that moment a young urchin ran round the side of the saloon and collided with the newcomers.

'Hold on there, boy,' chided Finn, smiling as he grabbed the kid by his skinny arms. 'Not so fast. How d'you fancy earnin' yourself a dime?'

The boy eyed him warily. 'Make it a quarter and yer on.'

Finn gave the kid a rueful shake of the head.

'You strike a hard bargain, mister.'

'Take it or leave it,' said the grubby kid curtly, pushing his hat to the back of his head and squaring his narrow shoulders.

Finn gave him the meanest look he could muster whilst trying not to smile.

'OK, you win,' he said after due consideration of the

offer. 'See that guy rifflin' the pasteboards in there?' He pointed out Paddy. 'Tell him the guntoter at the bar is Curly Joe Deakin. And not to reveal his presence at any cost. All he has to do is keep a close watch on the guy, and follow him if he leaves.'

The kid's eyes widened. This was serious, the stuff of dime novels. He moved off briskly towards the batwings.

Finn stayed him with a final warning. 'And no shootin' yer mouth off. That guy mustn't suspect a thing. OK?'

'Sure . . . sure thing, mister,' spluttered the kid eagerly.

'Now, before you go. Which is the best hotel in town?'

Without hesitation he replied, 'The Ranch House on North Street.'

'Tell the card-player that's where we're headin' now.'

Finn and Sarah watched tensely as the youngster approached Paddy. A few quick words were exchanged. Paddy's body stiffened perceptibly, his eyes shifting to the man at the bar, who had his back turned. Then he looked towards the door, saw Finn and gave a brief nod of under-standing.

The boy returned with his hand held palm upwards. Finn gave him two quarters. 'I may be needin' your help later,' he whispered, affecting a conspiratorial mien. 'Now, take us to this hotel.'

Mouth agape, the boy nodded. His friends were not going to believe this.

Keeping their eyes peeled for any sign of Brubekker, they led their horses down Gunnison Avenue eventually making a left turn into North Street. The hotel was at the end of the block. It was clearly the largest building in town. Finn told their guide to remain outside and await further instructions. The boy nodded enthusiastically, then sat down on the front step, sucking on a candy bar.

Before passing through the grandiose portals of the hotel, Finn and Sarah dusted off the accumulation of trail dust from their clothes. Inside, the entrance lobby was lit by two enormous crystal chandeliers imported from Europe. Sarah noted that it was as plush as any hotel on Sacramento's principal Sundowner Boulevard. Sumptuous red-velvet curtains draped the windows; the walls were lined with the heaviest of flock wallpapers. And on the floor was a carpet so thick you almost had to wade through it.

Striving hard not to be overawed by the extravagant setting, Finn sauntered casually up to the reception desk. The clerk was busy with another guest, which gave Finn the opportunity to glance furtively at the check-in register.

He smiled inwardly. The last two bookings were for a Mr John Bakersfield – room 205, and a Mr Joseph Dawson – room 206 – Jack Brubekker and Joe Deakin! A glance at the key-rack showed that Brubekker's key was missing.

'Brubekker must be in his room,' Finn murmured out of the side of his mouth. 'We'll have to work fast to get the drop on him. Here's what I figure we should do.' His plan remained unspoken as the desk clerk turned his attention to the new guests.

'Can I help you?' His beaky nose poked at the ceiling. The black-pencil moustache quivered.

'Two rooms please,' answered Finn, adding brusquely, 'and we want them on the second floor at the back.'

The clerk sniffed superciliously noting their shabby attire. He checked the register, muttering inaudibly to himself.

'Cash in advance . . . for three days,' snapped Sarah with equal bluntness.

That was different. Anybody offering cash on the nail was always welcome irrespective of how they looked. The clerk quickly signed them in with one hand whilst sliding the greenbacks into the till with the other.

He handed over their room keys with a smarmy: 'Enjoy your stay.'

As they ascended the broad staircase Finn outlined his plan. There was no time to lose. The smooth lawyer might decide to leave his room at any minute. Inside Finn's room, they synchronized timepieces. His was a standard pocket-watch attached to a silver chain. His father had left it when he disappeared into the wide blue yonder and Finn's mother had passed it on when her eldest son had gone in search of their inheritance. Sarah sported one of those new fangled wrist timepieces. Finn smirked, thinking such a trend would never catch on.

'Remember!' insisted Finn, tapping the face of the watch. 'At exactly a quarter to five, you knock on Brubekker's door. Say you're the maid come to change the water. When he comes to answer it, that's when I make my move.'

'What if he calls for me to enter?' quizzed Sarah.

'Knock again. He must answer the door so his back is to the window.'

Sarah looked down at her watch. It read twenty minutes to five.

'Good luck,' she said with a catch in her throat. Reaching up she kissed him tenderly on the lips. 'There's more where that came from if we come out of this intact.'

Finn caught his breath, heart fluttering madly. Eyes

moist, he pulled her to him, returning the kiss with a fierce passion he had never before experienced.

'And if we don't?'

'Never say die!' Sarah's emotive comeback was barely above a whisper. 'The hospital motto in Sacramento. Believe it!'

Their eyes locked, their hands clasped together, Finn was rooted to the spot. It was Sarah who broke the spell. She guided him over to the window and raised the sash.

'Three minutes left.'

Finn climbed out after giving her one final peck on the cheek. Then he was moving, silent as a ghost, along the veranda. Lengthening shadows of early evening hid him from any prying eyes. Bending low he counted off three windows and stopped beside the fourth. This must be room 205. The curtains were still open.

As he peered through the dust-smeared glass, his gaze caught the edge of a bed round to the left. A booted leg lay dangling over the side. Brubekker must be having a lie down. Maybe he was even asleep, but Finn could not take the chance. He would wait for Sarah's knock. Even in the cool breeze, he felt a hot flush suffuse his entire body.

Sixteen minutes to the hour. He released the hammer thong and eased the revolver from its holster. The loud double click of the hammer sounded like a thunderclap to his heightened senses.

Then he heard it. *Rat-tat-tat!*

The leg remained still. Again, louder this time. *Rat-tat-tat-tat!*

This time he heard a boorish grunt.

'Who is it?'

'Maid service, sir,' came back Sarah's simple refrain.

'Can I change your water, sir?'

'Not now. Come back later.'

Finn stiffened. His hand tightened on the trigger. Was the dude gonna be awkward?

'Please, sir. I have to do it now or the manager will be angry.'

Silence. Then:

'Come in if you have to,' he moaned.

'I can't, sir. My hands is full. Could you open the door, please.'

More grumbling, then both legs appeared as their owner stood up. Brubekker stretched his cramped muscles and shuffled over to the door.

This was it.

FOURTEEN

CONFESSION

Brubekker's hand gripped the doorknob as Finn prepared to yank the sash up, praying that it wouldn't stick. The door swung open at the very moment that the window emitted a raucous squeak. Finn swung effortlessly into the room, his revolver aimed at Brubekker's back.

'One false move an' I'll fill yer scurvy hide full of lead.'

The lawyer was taken completely by surprise. He staggered back as the door was pushed firmly open. Used to thinking on his feet in court, Brubekker quickly recovered his poise.

'What is this outrage?' he blustered. 'How dare you come bursting in here. You won't get away with this. I'll have the law. . . .' He hesitated as recognition of his assailant slammed home. 'You!'

'That's right, *Mister* Brubekker,' Finn growled, unable to keep the anger from his voice. 'Thought I was swingin' from a rope by now, didn't you? Well I've come back from the dead to haunt you. And I aim to see you in the pokey

142

along with your murderin' partner.' He advanced on the sweating lawyer, pistol wavering ominously. 'Now, where have you stashed that gold nugget?'

'I don't know what you are talking about,' denied the lawyer, backing away yet still managing to adopt his best courtroom manner. 'And as for a gold nugget, you are completely on the wrong trail. I'm here in Purgatory on legal business.'

'It won't wash, Brubekker,' butted in Sarah, hands on hips, legs apart. 'My father wrote me about that nugget. He left a map as to its whereabouts in your safe-keeping. Paid for the trust and integrity that you betrayed.' Her face reddened as a rush of indignation threatened to extinguish her cool harangue of the scheming toad. 'Safe-keeping! Trust!' she sneered, launching herself at the man and punching him hard, full in the mouth with all her strength. His head snapped back, a thin trickle of red seeping from the twisted mouth. 'You and that Joe Deakin robbed him. And now that he's dead, killed by your partner, that nugget is mine.'

Brubekker was deflated. His jaw dropped.

'So you're Ezra's daughter. I never figured—'

'Too late,' she spat. 'You shouldn't have been so greedy. And now you will be up for murder along with that lowdown skunk propping up the bar in the saloon.'

'But I didn't kill anyone,' pleaded the lawyer, throwing up his hands. He dabbed at his mouth. 'It was Deakin who pulled the trigger.'

Finn laughed harshly. But the sound had a cold ring.

'As a lawyer you should know that accomplices are equally guilty in the eyes of the law.' Then he shrugged impatiently. 'Anyway, we ain't got time to bandy words with the likes of you. It's that weasel Deakin I'm after, to clear my name.' He handed Sarah the heavy six-shooter, to cover the lawyer whilst securing him to the bedstead, finishing with a bandanna fastened tightly round his mouth.

'Go over to the sheriff's office and tell him the full story,' he told Sarah. 'It'll go down better comin' from a woman.' He held up his hands defensively on perceiving her hackles rise. 'OK, OK. I know. But you gotta bury your pride for once. My life is at stake here. If I can't clear my name, it'll be the owl-hoot trail and a rope at the end of the line, fer sure.'

Her face softened. 'Sorry, Finn,' she murmured, 'You're right.'

'Bring the sheriff over here,' Finn went on. 'Then its up to me to persuade him of my innocence. Now off you go. We haven't much time. Deakin could arrive at any moment.'

Once she had left, Finn made himself comfortable in a chair. And waited for his plan to play out.

Outside, it was already dark. The street urchin jumped to his feet when Sarah appeared.

'Take me to the sheriff's office,' she instructed him. The incongruous pair made their way back to Gunnison Avenue. The sheriff's office was half-way down on the far side.

'Wait here for me,' she said. The kid pulled at her arm, hand extended. Her brow puckered but she dug in her pocket and extracted a dime. 'It's all I have on me,' she said curtly. This kid was mercenary. A sharp rap on the door was followed by a gruff reply to enter.

The relating of the bizarre train of events had to be

144

concise yet persuasive. The sheriff, a bluff, red-faced man in his mid-forties, going by the handle of Bill Pepper, listened without interruption. A head of thick, prematurely grey hair made him look ten years older. Struggling to keep order in a succession of rough frontier towns was enough to age any man. Bill Pepper had been more than happy to accept the job of sheriff in a sleepy town like Purgatory, where the occasional drunken spree on a Saturday night was the most he had had to contend with.

The story this girl had told him sounded as if it had been lifted from one of them lurid paperbacks that were all the rage. He shook his head, unable to comprehend what she had related.

'Are you certain about this?' His sceptical tone made her all the more determined.

'Of course I am. Are you accusing me of inventing the whole thing?' Sarah banged her fist on the desk, emphasizing her exasperation.

'It just seems so incredible.'

'If you will only come to the hotel now, I can prove that what I've told you is the truth, the whole truth and nothing but the truth,' she pleaded, injecting a note of legality into her request.

'I don't know . . .' he hesitated.

'What harm can it do?'

Pepper scratched his head, screwing up his lined face into a fraught grimace. He paced the office a couple of times, thinking hard, idly fingering the tin star pinned to his leather vest. Then he paused in mid-stride, studied the girl pensively from beneath bushy eyebrows, and nodded, having arrived at a decision.

'OK,' he said, facing this sassy young woman. 'But it

145

better not be a wild-goose chase, else I'll jail the pair of
you for wastin' my time.'

Sarah offered her most endearing smile, displaying a
perfect set of even white teeth. Quickly she ushered
Pepper outside and back up the street. Completely forgotten was the young messenger who tagged on behind. The
ragged-assed urchin sensed there was more money to be
made out of this situation. He hunkered down to await
developments on the steps outside the hotel entrance.

The sheriff hustled through the lobby and mounted the
stairs two at a time, with Sarah close behind. Even though
dubious as to the credibility of the weird sequence of
events recently brought to his attention, it had nonetheless stirred Pepper's curiosity. Outside room 205, he
paused, then knocked twice. The door was immediately
opened by a tall blond-haired fellow, a resolute composure
showing in his icy gaze. The hogleg in his right hand was
pointed at the sheriff's belly.

'This is Finn McCall,' announced Sarah, 'and that
trussed-up turkey is Dandy Jack Brubekker, the thieving
lawyer who stole my inheritance.'

'And you claim this man was holding on to a map that
indicated where your father had concealed a large gold
nugget,' stated Pepper, eyeing the untidy heap sprawled
across the bed.

'That's right.'

'He don't look so dandy now,' Pepper scoffed before
addressing his next remark to Finn. 'Would you mind
aiming that shooter somewhere else, mister.'

'Oh, sorry, Sheriff,' Finn apologized. He holstered the
sidearm before hurrying on: 'I'd be obliged if you would
go into the closet.' He indicated a small antechamber to

the right. 'Leave the door slightly ajar so you can hear everything that's said when this dude's accomplice arrives. Then you'll be sure it ain't no fairytale Sarah's been tellin' you.'

Bill Pepper appeared decidedly awkward. His brow knitted. This was highly irregular, unlike anything he had encountered previously in his dealings with the law. Reluctantly he complied. 'OK, Mr McCall, but this better be on the level.'

'It is, Sheriff. Believe me, it is,' Finn reassured him. Turning to Sarah he said, 'Go down to the lobby and tell that kid to go fetch Deakin. He should tell him his partner has some important news, and he's at the hotel in room 205.'

She was back in less than a minute. Her breath came in short gasps.

'Deakin's down in the lobby now, checking the room numbers,' she panted. 'Must have got tired of waiting on Brubekker and has come to check him out.'

Without replying, Finn shepherded her into the anteroom along with the sheriff. Clumping boots echoed outside in the corridor, growing louder as they approached room 205. The door swung open just as Finn managed to secrete himself behind it. Deakin stepped inside. His jaw dropped as he caught sight of his partner trussed up on the bed. Instinctively, his right hand dropped to the Schofield's ivory butt.

Finn was ready. 'Don't try it, Deakin, you're covered,' he snapped abrasively. 'Now reach!'

Slowly, Deakin raised his hands, swivelling his head to peer at his adversary.

'The sodbuster!' he exclaimed.

'That's right. Thought you'd done fer me, didn't you?'

'What yer doin' here?'

'I came to take you back to stand trial for murder.'

'Reckon you can make it stick, then?' smirked Deakin, unaware that others were listening in.

'Why not?' snarled Finn, waving his own pistol in Deakin's face. 'You shot Ezra Tindle and made sure I took all the blame.'

'Sure I did. Killed him when he wouldn't reveal where the nugget was hidden. But there ain't a jury in the whole of Colorado that would ever convict me without cast-iron proof.' Deakin uttered a coarse laugh and prodded a finger towards the tethered Brubekker. 'And he won't spill the beans. 'Cos it'll mean his neck gettin' stretched too. It's just your word agin mine.'

'That's where you're wrong, mister.' Bill Pepper pushed open the anteroom door to reveal himself, a Colt Frontiersman cocked and ready in his right hand. 'I found it difficult to believe that the events related by Miss Tindle about the death of her father were nothing more than a fairytale cooked up to save this young feller's hide.' He poked a thumb at Finn. 'But you've condemned yourself out of your own mouth and I'm placing you under arrest for murder in the first degree.'

Just as he was about to slap a pair of handcuffs on the culprit's wrists, Sarah dashed past and lunged at Deakin, lashing out with her hands in blind fury. The tension built up over the last few days had finally snapped. All the pain and anguish at the loss of her father to this murdering coyote bubbled over. Pummelling his brawny frame with her tiny fists, the two of them backed across the room with Deakin fending her off as best he could.

And that was the moment Paddy McCall chose to enter the fray. Having witnessed Deakin finish his drink abruptly and leave the saloon, he had followed some fifty yards behind. Not knowing which room the skunk had entered, he was forced to listen carefully at the top of the landing before raised voices drew him to number 205.

He slammed open the door and barged in, thinking his brother was in trouble. Finn was knocked off balance as the door struck his gun hand. The pistol flew off into a corner and slithered under the bed as Finn staggered against the dresser, wildly trying to keep his feet.

Paddy stared. He took in the girl wrestling with Deakin, Jack Brubekker trussed up and gagged on the bed, and Sheriff Bill Pepper staring open-mouthed like a stranded fish; it all combined to blur his vision of reality. What was happening here?

The stunned hestitancy was enough for Curly Joe. He grabbed his revolver and fanned the hammer. Flame spat twice from the gun barrel. The noise was deafening in the confines of the small room. The first slug shattered a mirror in the anteroom door. An instant later, Paddy cried out, clutching at his right leg. He spun round crashing into the sheriff, blood spurting from the wound. Both of them tumbled on to the floor. Only Finn remained on his feet, and he was unarmed.

Where a carefully orchestrated plan resulting in due process of the law had been enacted seconds previously, all was now in uproar. Deakin took full advantage of the chaotic mêlée. He slung an arm round Sarah's neck, hugging her to his chest, the deadly barrel of the Schofield poking at her cheek.

'Don't nobody move a muscle,' howled Deakin, a wild

manic gleam in his eyes. To emphasize his command of the situation, he jabbed the pistol hard into Sarah's face. She gave an anguished whimper. 'I'm leavin' here now, and I'm takin' the girl with me.' He began shuffling sideways towards the door. 'Anybody follows and you know what'll happen.' A rancorous growl from deep within his throat left them in no doubt as to the fate of the girl should they try anything stupid.

Thrashing about on the bed, Brubekker had managed to dislodge the gag round his mouth.

'You can't leave me here. We had a deal,' he croaked.

Deakin scowled disdainfully at his partner in crime. His mouth twisted into a baleful leer.

'I should never have gotten involved with the likes of you. Look what's happened.' Quick as a snapping 'gator, the gun flashed. Brubbeker jerked as the bullet struck him in the chest. His body arched. A choking retch accompanied the deathly convulsions before he slumped, a crimson stain spreading evenly across his vest, adding to its garish allure.

Sarah emitted a piercing shriek, choked off by Deakin's rough hold on her. Another place, another killing. Could you become immune to such occurrences? She shook her head. Death was an everyday part of life in her profession. But this was different. The brutish violence was something nobody should ever take for granted, except vicious killers like the one now threatening her own existence.

Outside in the corridor, a hum of activity announced that the crash of gunfire had not gone unnoticed. Doors squeaked open as other guests peered out of their rooms, anxiously trying to determine the cause of the uproar.

'Keep back, I said,' repeated Deakin. More than a hint

of panic inflected his raised utterance as he realized he had to make a rapid exit if he was to escape. The nugget was forgotten as the instinctive human urge for survival pounded his brain. 'One step closer and the girl gets it.'

Finn drew back, fearing for her safety. Now that he had found the one person he truly cared for, Finbar McCall had no intention of seeing her taken from him.

'You might as well surrender, kid,' advised Sheriff Pepper stoically. 'You ain't goin' no place.'

'That so,' snarled Deakin. He wrenched open the door into the corridor. Instantly, a chorus of other doors slammed shut as guests sought the sanctuary of their own rooms, the proverb concerning the fate of a certain curious cat obviously in their minds. 'Now move out of the way or else the filly gets it.' There was no disputing his resolve. 'You go first, Sheriff, and clear a way through the lobby. And make certain everybody down there knows the score.'

Sweat rolled down Curly Joe's blotchy face. His hands were shaking. Pepper knew this was the most dangerous moment in any stand-off, and he'd faced down numerous killers in the past. One false move could see that wavering shooter blazing hot lead.

'Easy there,' he said quietly. 'Nobody's gonna stop you.' That would come later. But he left that thought unspoken. Then turning to Finn he added, 'You stay here and see to your brother, Mr McCall. That wound needs a doctor.'

As the bizarre group backed down the stairway, patrons of the hotel scattered under the hoarse directions of the sheriff. Outside, tied to the hitching rail, were a pair of fine matching greys attached to a well-kept buggy.

'We'll take this,' rapped Deakin. He ordered the girl to mount up. 'You stay inside and keep that door closed,' he said, giving Pepper a cold glare.

Once the sheriff had disappeared back into the Ranch House, Deakin swung the loaded pistol and raked the front of the hotel with the remaining bullets. Glass panels shattered inwards and he was pleased to see those inside diving for cover. He grabbed up the reins in one hand and a whip in the other and lashed at the grey rumps. The frightened animals reared up under the fierce onslaught. Another withering crack of the whip and they bounded off down the street, the girl clinging precariously to the fancy awning.

Once he deemed the coast was clear, Sheriff Pepper emerged from the wrecked frontage of the Ranch House followed closely by a distraught Finn McCall. Both had guns drawn, but their quarry had disappeared.

Which direction had he taken? It was now totally dark, the moon obscured by thick cloud, and there was nobody on North Street who would have seen.

Nobody except for a thin youngster squatting on the steps idly tossing a coin in his hand.

Finn approached him.

'Did you see which way that buggy went?' His tone was strained edgy with impatience. The boy continued flicking the coin, a cheeky smirk on his dirty face. He looked at the coin suggestively. With a furious snarl Finn grabbed the kid by his overalls and slammed him hard up against the wall of the hotel. 'I won't ask again, you scrawny runt,' he hissed, spittle flecking the kid's cowering features.

'A-all right, a-all right,' stammered the terrified boy, stabbing a finger towards the west. 'They went down North Street, then took a left heading for the old Ute trail.'

Finn let the youngster go, his flash of temper dissipating. 'Sorry about that, kid,' he apologized, offering the boy a silver dollar. 'But that guy has a heap to answer for and the sooner I git on his trail, the better.'

The kid's eyes bulged. 'Gee, thanks mister,' he gushed. He hurried away into an adjacent alley – just in case the tetchy stranger decided to change his mind.

But Finn was already considering the implications of Deakin's flight.

'That guy is hell-bent on trouble if'n he tries to go through the cut-off,' cautioned Pepper, tugging at his dark moustache, 'and not just because he's pushin' a buggy.'

Finn nodded sagely.

'The Ute Revenge?'

'That's it,' agreed Pepper, eyeing the younger man quizzically. 'You know of it?'

'We came through that way from Telluride. Almost became a tribal sacrifice.'

Pepper was about to ask more questions when Finn stopped him with a raised hand.

'I'll tell you the full story when I've rescued Sarah,' he said, striding over to the chestnut.

'Want me to come with you?' asked Pepper, placing a restraining hand on the horse's bridle.

'Much obliged, Sheriff. But this is something I have to do on my own.'

Pepper gave a curt nod of understanding. 'You can beat him to the canyon by taking a short cut by way of Crested Butte. A single rider on a horse can make it. Deakin will have to go the long way round in a buggy. You oughta be able to catch him out in the open.'

Concise instructions were followed by a brief smile of thanks. Tapping his wide-brimmed Texan against the rump of the chestnut, Finn streaked away into the dusky gloom.

'Good luck!' The sheriff's final call accompanied him round a bend and out on to the dark flatlands beyond.

FIFTEEN

PAYBACK

In the dense opacity of night, Finn allowed his mount to pick its own trail through the loose scattering of boulders at the lower edge of the mesa country once he'd left the Gunnison River behind. Transitory appearances of the moon provided much needed light for him to pick out the tortuous track beside Crested Butte on to the plateau lands behind. He hoped that Deakin was likewise struggling on the low-level route. Round about two in the morning, Finn was forced though sheer exhaustion to take a rest. Had he carried on, like as not he would have tumbled out of the saddle.

For three hours, Finn catnapped beneath his blanket in the shelter of an overhang. At night the winds blowing across high mountain terrain could cement a man to the cold rocks. Even in the height of summer there was no respite.

At the first hint of dawn, Finn was on the move again. He chewed on a tough piece of jerked beef left in his saddle-bags from a previous expedition. Washed down with a mouthful of water from his half-empty canteen, it would have to be sufficient. His body was running on pure adrenaline. Real food would have to wait.

Around noon, he spotted the entrance to the canyon leading out of the San Miguel cut-off. Had it only been the previous day that the three riders had hot-hoofed out of that deadly chasm? He settled himself on a shelf overlooking the approach. The sun was rising into a cloudless sky. It was going to be a hot day. He checked that the long-barrelled Henry was fully loaded and laid it out on the rock slab, then did the same with his Navy Colt. Pulling his hat-brim down to shade out the glare, he squinted back up the dusty trail. To while away the time, he pulled out a cheroot and lit up.

He didn't have long to wait.

A low plume of dust rose from the desert floor. Deakin had made good time. Maybe he hadn't even stopped. Fear of the hangman's rope lent impetus to a man's actions. Quickly Finn stubbed out the cigar. No sense advertising his presence. But where was Sarah? Not perched on the swaying bench seat beside Deakin, that was for sure. Had he killed her already? Finn's blood boiled, his fists clenched white.

Then he saw her leg poking out behind. She must be on the bed of the wagon. Probably tied up. Sucking in a deep draught of oxygen, he settled the rosewood stock of the rifle against his stubbly chin and took aim, carefully drawing back the hammer.

Holding off until the buggy was within a hundred yards, he gently squeezed the trigger. The loud report bounced off the surrounding rocks as the stock recoiled into his shoulder. An agonizing barb hammered up his arm. Grimacing back the wave of pain threatening to engulf him, he had the satisfaction of witnessing Deakin lift off the buggy and plummet into the sand. A grim smile split Finn's leathery features.

It was payback time!

On hearing the rifle crack, Sarah levered herself into a sitting position to see Finn emerging from his place of concealment. Tears in her eyes, she blurted out cries of relief.

'Oh Finn, I thought I'd never see you again. Deakin said he was going to leave me stranded in this god-forsaken wilderness as soon as he felt safe from pursuit.'

After removing the bonds from her hands and feet, Finn took her in his arms and kissed her gently. She responded with fervour. Then, for a brief instant, she pulled away.

'How did you manage to overtake us?' she asked, looking deep into his hooded eyes. Finn was about to reply when he saw a reflection embedded in her own green pools of light. It was only a momentary flicker, but sufficient to warrant desperate measures.

Unceremoniously, he thrust Sarah to the left, then drove his boot heels into the sand. Diving to the right, he twisted his body, grabbing at the holstered revolver. A shot rang out, the hot lead fanning his ear. Sprawled on the ground, he snapped off a couple of rapid shots. Only one struck its target, but that was enough.

Deakin clutched his chest, tottered a few steps, his face screwed up in surprise, then pitched forward on to his face. The body twitched once then lay still, unmoving. Finn breathed hard. The tension of having escaped certain death by the skin of his teeth was etched across his taut face.

Sarah stumbled to her feet and ran to him, arms outstretched.

For what seemed like an hour, but was no more than five minutes, she hugged him close. Nerves strained to breaking point, each needed the reassuring proximity of the other before anything like normality could be resumed.

Nearby, the two greys casually flicked cavorting flies with their tails. Tall yuccas swayed in the light breeze. A wandering sidewinder in search of a meal slithered by, its forked tongue probing the heat source. Uncertain of its intended prey, the reptile backed off and disappeared under a rock. Just another day in the desert.

At last Finn raised his head. He peered down at the bloody stain on his shirt sleeve.

'That wound has reopened,' he announced, biting on his lower lip to ease the throbbing ache. 'So that's another shirt ruined.'

Sarah smiled. 'I'll buy you a whole drawful of new shirts once the nugget's been sold.'

'I'd plumb forgotten all about that.'

'You'll be needing professional attention for that wound,' continued Sarah, gently easing back the open neck of the shirt. Gently she helped him up on to the buggy.

'Could be that my condition requires a more permanent solution.'

Sarah noted the wry smile, the perky lift of the eyebrows. 'What do you have in mind, Mr McCall?' she answered coyly, a slight hint of rouge suffusing her cheeks.

Finn laid his cards on the table. 'I had intended sellin' up the family legacy once I reached the lower Gunnison.' His soft gaze held her eyes. 'Now I ain't so sure. According to the lawyer back home, it would make a mighty fine home to settle down in, raise horses and cattle . . .' He paused, diffidently lowering his gaze. '. . . and maybe other things. In time, of course, once we've gotten to know each other,' he hurried on looking away to hide his embarrassment.

'All in good time, Finn,' she responded lightly. 'First you need to arrange for Sheriff Pepper to provide a written testimony to clear your name with the law back in Telluride. We'll not say anything about the saloon worker who mysteriously vanished.'

'Who told you about that?' Finn asked in surprise.

'The sheriff in Telluride said he'd suddenly quit town in mysterious circumstances.'

She waited for Finn to elaborate.

'It was self-defence. The guy pulled a gun,' he said, 'Paddy had no choice when he threatened to put the kibosh on our plans to break out of jail. We hid his body in a ravine.'

'Erm,' she murmured reflectively, 'I'll take your word for it.' Climbing up beside the man she had suddenly found herself desperately caring about, Sarah threw a careless glance towards the corpse splayed out on the desert floor.

'What about him?' she asked.

Finn considered a moment then, in a voice in which loathing and relief were combined, declared casually: 'Let the buzzards enjoy their lunch.'

What sounded very much like a guttural cheer burst

from the throats of a dozen winged spectators circling about that lonely place. Sarah idly glanced aloft. A soft glow of satisfaction had replaced the anxiety of recent times. Flicking the reins, the young couple left the scavengers to clear up the mess.